Shadow of
Dark Water

Shadow of Dark Water

Elizabeth Elgin

ROBERT HALE · LONDON

© Elizabeth Elgin 1978
This edition 1998

ISBN 0 7090 6268 0

Robert Hale Limited
Clerkenwell House
Clerkenwell Green
London EC1R OHT

The right of Elizabeth Elgin to be identified
as author of this work has been asserted by her
in accordance with the Copyright, Designs
and Patents Act 1988.

2 4 6 8 10 9 7 5 3 1

Printed in Great Britain by
St Edmundsbury Press Limited, Bury St Edmunds, Suffolk.
Bound by WBC Book Manufacturers Limited, Bridgend.

One

The road stretched ahead like narrow, white tape. On either side, slate-covered hills reached up from grassy slopes and the twilight that purpled their tips made them even more sombre, more aloof.

Petra Cunningham drove carefully, negotiating the steep bends with skill, a small smile tilting the corners of her mouth. She enjoyed sitting behind the wheel of a car, in spite of Simon's disapproval.

"Women don't make good drivers," he grumbled, loudly and often, to which remark she always wrinkled her nose and smiled. Simon couldn't help being the way he was. If she married him, she supposed, she would be cared for and protected for the rest of her life. More than once he had asked her.

"You know we suit each other," he had said, "and I can afford a wife."

It was over two years ago that they had first met and really, she thought, there was no reason at all why they shouldn't marry.

"The Agency is doing well, Petra my love. What's holding you back?"

What indeed, she wondered. Certainly Simon's advertising business, which promoted several small but popular products, was reasonably well established. The really big accounts still eluded him, but he was unashamedly ambitious and worked long and hard. Simon, Petra was forced to admit, would make a kind, considerate husband, but suiting each other was not enough and she did not care, either, for being afforded whispered the small voice of her conscience. She needed to love him deeply, to be in love with him, too. Crazily, inexplicably in love.

"And I'm not at all sure if I am," she whispered to the gathering gloom, for Simon had never touched her the way her body ached to be touched, never openly desired her. So here she was, maddeningly uncertain, driving alone through the Welsh mountains on a late afternoon in April. She had never been to Wales before and already the character of the landscape thrilled and excited her. Between twin peaks she could see the dim outline of the early rising moon, and through the open window of the car the air was fresh and keen and her ears rang slightly as the road climbed higher. On each side the great masses of slate seemed to press in as if, she thought with a tingle of apprehension, even the stones were curious about her. Since turning off from Betws-y-Coed, she had passed no other traffic and the slight breeze she noticed only a few miles back had dropped, giving way to a strange, watching stillness.

"Nonsense!" she jerked.

Her voice sounded odd in her ears and in the driving mirror her eyes looked wide and faintly alarmed. Deep brown and long-lashed with an upward tilt at the corners, they were her only real claim to beauty, she admitted, her wide mouth and pointed chin being well beyond redemption. Simon said she should make more of what she had, but Simon was a perfectionist who —

Petra slammed on her brakes with alarm as the road swooped down abruptly into a thick curtain of mist that had arisen so suddenly that it was as unbelievable as it was frightening. Something moved ahead of her. She had an impression of bulk and swung the wheel instinctively. There was a grinding sound as the car left the road and crunched over stones and then, as she came to a jerking halt, an ominous squelch.

"*Now* what have I done?"

Her exclamation was one of annoyance mingled with relief, for at least she was still in one piece. She opened the door and stepped out cautiously.

Her shoes sank into muddy grass and in the fading light she could see a low-lying meadow from which white mist arose and drifted towards her.

Walking round to the back of the car, she bit her lip in vexation. The rear wheels were settled firmly in the marshy ground and she knew she could not get the car onto the road again without help. And she didn't relish, either, spending the rest of the night huddled on the back seat. It was growing steadily colder, too, and the mist wreathed round in oddly contorted shapes. Behind her, something lurched across the stones and she turned quickly, heart hammering, in time to see a large sheep emerge from the surrounding haze, gaze at her steadily, then shamble away again. Probably, Petra thought with relief, it was a sheep that had caused her to swerve off the road in the first place. It was unlike her to react so impulsively, but she had been driving for several hours, she realised, and perhaps she was more tired than she realised.

For a moment, she considered sounding the horn for help, then shrugged away the thought with a whispered "Stupid!" But the rapidly gathering darkness was making her uneasy and there seemed nothing for it but to scramble back to the road and start walking. Roads always led somewhere, didn't they, and she was surely not too far from a village? Opening the car door she reached for the heavy coat that lay over the front seat. With its big collar turned up she felt warmer and cautious optimism arose inside her as she shook the folds from the road-map and tried to pinpoint her position.

The nearest village, she was almost certain, was about three miles away, but surely there would be a farm nearer than that?

Taking a torch from beneath the dashboard, she shone it around. As if on cue, the mist lifted, its ragged edges parting and in the distance another light shone steadily. Letting go a sob of relief, she was able to make out the shape of a house, stark against the lowering clouds that gathered on the horizon, before the mist drifted around again.

There would be people at the house who would help her and if she could pick her way across the fields, surely she could get there before it became completely dark?

Carefully she locked the car doors, though it seemed a needless precaution. Her torch was neither new nor particularly powerful, and she mentally crossed her fingers as she walked forward into the thick blanket that clung damply to her head and shoulders. The thin stream of light from the torch was miserably inadequate, but when she switched it off, the mist seemed even heavier and her own breathing too loud in her ears.

Her feet splashed suddenly into icy water that covered the tops of her shoes. She stopped dead, catching her breath in a gasp. The wavering light of her torch revealed the gleam of black water, but it was impossible to tell how far it stretched, or how deep it was. As she hesitated, a soft, squelching sound came faintly, muffled and distorted, but most certainly footsteps. Something – or someone – was walking towards her.

Petra tensed and the light of her torch flickered weakly and died. She stood rigid and apprehensive, shrouded by mist, her mouth opened to call out. But no sound came and suddenly she was blinded by a stronger light and a voice, deep and masculine said softly,

"Is it you, then? Are you come back ...?"

She could see only a dark shape that seemed to have risen up out of the ground, but whoever stood there was certainly a solid human being.

Gulping with relief, Petra found her voice again, though it shook with cold.

"I'm lost, I'm afraid. I was trying to get to the house up on the hill."

"By walking on water, I suppose?" The voice changed, becoming roughly sarcastic.

He lowered the lantern in whose glare she was trapped and stepped closer. His features were still shadowed, but Petra had an impression of height and intense masculinity.

"My car swerved off the road," she said, a ripple of annoyance running through her. "A sheep or something ran in front – "

"You didn't hit it?" he interrupted, sharply.

"I don't think so – no, I'm *sure* I didn't, but my car is bogged down in the mud. I got a brief glimpse of light through the mist and saw the house – "

"*My* house," he interrupted again. "What possessed you to try to reach it by this way?"

"Because the road seemed to go in the opposite direction, and the mist is so thick I couldn't think of anything better to do. And just in case you're interested," she flung, "I'm standing over my shoe-tops in freezing water!"

"Then you're lucky you haven't drowned," he returned harshly. "The ground slopes down very sharply without any warning a few yards further out and you'd have been up to your neck. The mist comes down so quickly over the pass that it's sheer stupidity to wander about in these parts."

"I'm not doing this for fun," she snapped, her voice trembling with tears as she moved carefully back onto the drier ground. "I told you, my car is stuck. I shall need a tow."

"Where are you going?"

"A place called *Ty Mawr*. It's a house."

"I know it." His voice was still impatient and he had thrust his head forward and was peering at her intently.

"Is it far from here?" she demanded, uneasily.

"About a couple of miles. Over in the next valley."

"How will I get there?"

"W-e-ll, I could give you a lift," he said, reluctantly. "The car's up at the farm. I suppose you'd better come with me, Miss Cunningham."

"You know my name?"

She forgot the discomforts of wet feet and intense cold as she stared at him.

"I know you are expected."

He put out his hand and caught her own slim fingers in a grasp that was unexpectedly warm and reassuring, though his voice remained curt.

"My name is Gareth Davies. Your uncle was a neighbour of mine."

"Great-uncle," she corrected, stumbling over the uneven ground. "Ifor Jones was my grandmother's brother."

"Grand old man. Pity you couldn't be bothered to pay your respects at the funeral!"

"I didn't even know he had died until his solicitors got in touch with me a few weeks back," she retorted, indignantly. "My grandmother cut herself off from her family when she married, I was told, but my mother used to write to her Uncle Ifor," she defended. "Then, when she died, my father wrote and told him about it, but there was no reply. I heard nothing after that until the solicitors sent for me."

She broke off, gasping as the ground began to slope sharply upward.

"You'd better save your breath," Gareth Davies said, dryly. "The going gets rougher from now on."

As she struggled after him, up into the mist, Petra thought wryly that her great-uncle's neighbour was not behaving in a very neighbourly manner. In spite of the warmth of his hand, he was making it very clear that he considered her to be nothing more than a very great nuisance.

On the higher ground the mist began to thin. A wall loomed ahead of them and a large dog bounded through the open gate, barking on a high, excited note.

"Down, Gyp! Down!" Gareth Davies ordered sharply and the dog dropped to its haunches, grumbling softly.

"He's lovely!" Impulsively Petra held out her hand.

"Best not try to stroke him. Gyp isn't used to foreigners," came the gruff warning. "My car's at the side. I'll get it out if you wait here."

"But I'm wringing wet!"

Regaining her breath, she snatched her hand from his and rounded on him, her frustration bubbling over.

"Surely you can invite me in for a few minutes to warm myself a little!"

"I'm not one for visitors," he shrugged, "but you can come in if you want to ..."

"Thank you!" she gasped, her voice thick with sarcasm.

He answered with a snort that could have been either amusement or derision and led the way across a cobbled yard to the side of the house, where he pushed open a door.

The passage in which she found herself led into a long, low room with whitewashed walls and dark beams. A lantern, similar to the one Gareth Davies carried, stood on the sill of the uncurtained window, the light, she realised, that she had glimpsed through the mist from the track below. A fire glowed on the hearth and gleams of slate were exposed between the sheepskin rugs that covered the floor.

Gareth Davies hung up the lantern on a hook in the ceiling then turned to face her. He was certainly above average height, his shoulders broad under a greatcoat of dark cloth. Mist had damped his thick black hair into a frizz of curls that overhung his broad, weather-tanned forehead. Eyes of a darker brown than her own stared down at her without friendliness and the corner of his mobile mouth quirked downward as he studied her frankly.

"You look like a drowned rat," he said, flatly.

"That wasn't what you thought when you first saw me," Petra challenged. "You thought I was somebody else, didn't you? You said – "

"What I said is of no consequence," he returned, harshly. "If you go through there you'll find hot water and towels. Take one of the lanterns with you. We don't run to electric light, up here."

"I thought you had all the modern conveniences in Wales," she said.

"Most people have, but I prefer things as they are. I'll put the kettle on ..."

It was a dismissal. Cheeks burning, Petra accepted the lantern in silence and walked into the next room. Evidently, it was where Gareth Davies slept, she pondered, even though she had noticed an upper storey with two shuttered windows. It was a smaller room, clean and whitewashed as the other one, with a narrow brass-railed bed against one wall and an immense wardrobe against the other. Here, too, the floor was of slate and the only ornaments were a group of silver cups, arranged on a shelf over the unlit fire. Another shelf held a long row of books and a pile of tattered farming journals. There was a washbasin in the corner with towels hung over a rail at the side.

Petra kicked off her wet, muddy shoes, hung her damp coat over the foot of the bed and stripped off her tights. They dripped water onto the floor and her toes were soaking. Her shoes, she thought ruefully, were completely ruined.

The water that gushed hot from the bright brass tap was a welcome surprise. A bath, she thought longingly, would have been bliss, but it was obvious that Gareth Davies was not the sort to give unwelcome strangers the run of his bathroom, even supposing he had one.

From the other room he called,

"You can borrow a pair of socks from the top drawer of the chest, if you like. And there's an old pair of wellingtons out here."

"Thank you. That's very kind," she called back.

The socks were far too big, but they were handknitted from homespun wool and were beautifully, comfortingly warm. She wriggled her toes luxuriously and towelled her wet hair. Taking a comb, she leaned closer to the small mirror to tidy the fine strands of hair that hung limply about her face. Soon, she would be twenty-three, she considered, yet she looked more like a fifteen-year old waif.

"A drowned rat indeed," she muttered, scowling at her reflection.

Yet Simon thought she was beautiful. No woman he knew, he often said, had such fine bone-structure as she, yet this big, curly-haired Welshman treated her as if she were nothing better than a nuisance.

She rummaged in her bag for a lipstick and defiantly applied it with a heavier hand than usual. At least she now looked more presentable, not, she told herself firmly, that it mattered in the slightest what the Welshman thought.

Carefully she folded the wet towels and rinsed the washbasin. The room, neat as it was, was obviously the room of a bachelor. There were none of the small, feminine touches that a wife would have added. Even the books on the shelf were mainly collections of detective stories and political biographies. Only one, a volume of Dylan Thomas's poetry, hinted at more literary tastes. She drew out the slender book and fanned through its pages. Here and there, a line had been heavily underscored.

'*Rage, rage against the dying of the light,*' was one such line and in the margin at the side, the same hand had written the one word, '*Eleri*'.

But it was none of her business what books Gareth Davies read or who wrote in their margins. Feeling a little ashamed, she put the book back hastily, slipped her coat around her shoulders and went back into the other room.

"There's tea if you want it," her unwilling host said, nodding towards a small table. "Help yourself to the bara brith."

The bara brith, Petra discovered, was a thickly-sliced loaf, solid with dried fruit and candied peel and plentifully buttered. Gratefully she munched a piece and drank a large cup of strong, sweet tea. He did not, she noticed, invite her to sit down but strode out into the side-passage while she was eating and came back with a pair of wellingtons.

"Megan Pritchard will be over to *Ty Mawr* in the morning, I shouldn't wonder," he said, watching her pull them on. "Her brother has a tow, so if you let her know, she'll get him to pull your car onto the road again."

"Is *Ty Mawr* locked up, then?"

"Yes, but Megan goes up most days to see that it's all right. She's been expecting you for weeks, ever since old Ifor died. She used to clean and cook for him. With him for years ..."

"I hope she won't be disappointed, then, because I'm not sure if I'll be staying very long," Petra hesitated. "I work in an office, you see, and it's only now that I've been able to get some time off."

"You'll have a key to the house, Miss Cunningham?"

"Yes," she nodded. "The solicitor gave one to me. But isn't there a pub or somewhere I could stay for tonight?"

"Now see here. I've no time to go driving around the countryside looking for bed and board for you," he replied testily. "The car's ready when you are. On guard, Gyp!"

Subdued yet seething, Petra followed him into the yard again, the boots clumping inelegantly. They were far too big, but at least they were dry and her feet were warm again. He had not seemed to notice her improved appearance but, as he opened the door of a small, battered car he said,

"You ought not to cut your hair. Women should have long hair ..."

He said it gruffly, his eyes averted.

"And tiny waists and lace fans, I suppose," she retorted lightly, but he merely grunted, slammed the door shut and went round to the driving seat, bending himself into it without another glance in her direction.

As they drove out of the yard, she could not help questioning nervously,

"Is there—will there be electric light at *Ty Mawr*?"

"Not for foreigners," he returned. "It's not the main road, you know. Just a track that connects the two valleys. Safe enough if you follow the curve of the pass."

"Is there – will there be electric light at Ty Mawr?"

"Oh, yes. Old Ifor was a great one for the improvements. Central-heating, television – he got the lot in. Like toys they were to him. 'Come and have a look at my new toaster,' he said to me one day and over I went, and watched him make enough toast to feed the whole of Gwynedd."

"You were fond of him," Petra stated.

"We got on very well," he acknowledged, "for all that he was well past seventy and more than twice my age."

"Two bachelors together," she said, lightly, but he merely clamped his mouth shut, as if regretting the momentary dropping of his guard and scowled ahead into the mist, his hands firm on the wheel. Her own hand inadvertently touched the edge of his coat and she moved away slightly, aware that his presence disturbed her though she could not have told exactly why.

"The wind is getting up. It'll shift the mist," he said, abruptly.

Certainly the mist was thinning, for now Petra could make out the rough track along which they were slowly driving and for one brief moment the moon emerged, its pale-blue light throwing into relief the black mountains that reared up starkly on each side of them.

"This is the highest point. We drop down, now, into the next valley. *Ty Mawr* is built at the side of the river."

"Are there other houses?"

"A couple of farms, but the village itself is at the head of the valley. There are one or two scattered cottages, as well. The quarrymen lived in them once, but the slate's all gone, now."

"I shall enjoy exploring," she said.

"Looking over your estate? Fraternising with the natives?"

There was no mistaking the enmity in his voice, now.

"I'm surprised you could bear to have waited so long, Miss Cunningham, before taking possession."

"Of the house?"

She stole a glance at his unyielding profile.

"Of the entire property. Surely you know what you inherited?" he said, impatiently.

"Yes, of course I do. The property known as *Ty Mawr*," she replied, puzzled.

"Miss Cunningham, your great-uncle owned *all* the land in this valley," he said. "Over fifteen-hundred acres of it, and that includes most of the village. You're a very rich young woman. Ah, there's the big house. You can see it, through the trees."

He nodded ahead and she leaned forward, anticipation quivering through her as they dropped down into a blackness from which tall chimneys rose up like silent, moon-tinted sentinels.

"*Ty Mawr*," she whispered, and the name tripped off her tongue like music, "It's mine – really mine ... "

Two

They drove slowly between high posts on which the car headlights gleamed briefly.

"This is the house," Gareth Davies said, bringing the car to a halt. "Do you have the key?"

"In my bag." She rummaged for it, aware of his gaze. "Will you come in and show me where the lights are?"

It hurt her pride to have to ask another favour of him, but he seemed not to notice and nodded his head briefly.

Ty Mawr appeared to be larger than she had expected, but it was difficult to see its outline properly, so complete was the darkness around them.

She stumbled, and felt his hand under her elbow and an odd little tremor quivered along her nerves again, irritating her because momentarily she had found it pleasing.

The big key turned easily in the lock and the heavy door swung inwards.

"The switches are here at the side," he said, stepping ahead of her and pressing them down.

The hall flooded with light, blinding her for an instant, then she blinked around a wide, slate-floored space with a staircase curving up to an ornately-carved gallery.

The air about her had the chill of disuse and thick walls held in the silence.

"The living-rooms are down there," Gareth offered, leaning his head to the left. "Kitchen quarters the other side, bedrooms above. You'll not be nervous, here alone?"

"No. Of course not."

She spoke defiantly, annoyed by the mockery in his voice. His eyes held hers for an instant, then he shrugged and said,

"I'll be getting back, then. Megan will be here in the morning ..."

He nodded briskly then opened the door, half turning to wish her goodnight.

The tail-lights of his car glowed briefly and receded. Tendrils of mist were reaching into the hall through the open door, but she waited until the sound of the engine had died away before she banged it shut and slid home the bolts.

She stood for a moment listening to the silence then walked resolutely beneath the curved archway and down the passage of polished slate.

The boots Gareth Davies had given her clumped and thudded with every step. Clucking impatiently, she stepped out of them, placing them side by side in the nearest doorway.

She curled her toes as she walked, for stockinged feet on the zealously-polished floor made progress hazardous. Perhaps, she thought, if she stayed at *Ty Mawr*, she might cover the passages and hallway. Rush-matting would blend well, she decided impulsively, and would deaden the empty, hollow sound of footfalls. And the house *was* empty and hollow. *Ty Mawr* was lonely; lonely for people who could make it into a home, and it seemed to Petra that it was watching her with unseen eyes, wondering, waiting ...

She coughed nervously and opened the door to her left,

feeling for the light-switch, gasping with pleasure as the room was flooded with soft light.

It was a large apartment that was surprisingly cosy. Warm-beige carpeting covered the floor, and chintz-upholstered chairs and sofas were grouped informally around the open stone hearth.

Flowers, thought Petra. Masses of flowers and firelight dancing on the copper jugs and brasses. The room would come alive, then.

She tried to conjure up a Christmas scene, with holly-smothered beams, a tinsel-strung tree and children, Simon's children, sitting by the fireside. But it refused to materialise and she saw instead a dog named Gyp, sprawled before the grate and a Welshman in homespun socks with toes that curled with pleasure in the warmth of crackling logs.

"Ha!" she jerked out loud, impatiently dismissing so improbable a picture. She shrugged derisively. Gareth Davies, indeed!

The dining-room was formal with black oak and time-seasoned elm and prints of nineteenth century racehorses. The table was long and narrow and set with pewter and a red-Turkey carpet contrasted pleasantly with the white-painted walls.

Through an archway at the far end, she found a smaller, book-lined room, with leather armchairs set on either side of a copper-clad fireplace and dotted with small tables and green-shaded lamps. A pipe-rack hung on the chimney-breast and a tobacco jar stood on the hearth.

Was this your favourite room, Uncle Ifor? Petra mused. Did you sit here by the fire with your books and your pipe on long winter evenings? Did Gareth Davies visit you and did you listen to music, together?

Gareth Davies! Get out of my hair. Ty Mawr is mine, now, and there is no place in it for tall, surly Welshmen!

At the end of the corridor, double doors opened onto a long, narrow room, its uncurtained windows reaching from floor to ceiling, its empty fireplace bright with old-fashioned Dutch tiles in clear, sharp blues. It was an enchanting room, a room for children to use as their own, a day-nursery, a den. One day, a fire would glow in the hearth and socks would hang to warm on a brass-edged fireguard. There would be the marks of small, sticky fingers on the paintwork, toys scattered about the floor ...

She was dreaming again. The room in which she stood was a storeroom, stacked with boxes and pieces of hi-fi equipment, old leather suitcases, a tape-recorder, and she, Petra Cunningham, seemed to have fallen under the spell of the valley. She was becoming light-headed and romantic and completely stupid!

Across the hall were two empty rooms and a long, shiny kitchen. Her great-uncle, she thought with a tinge of amusement, had certainly had a passion for gadgets. This was not the kitchen she had hoped to find. There were no copper pans, no kitchen dresser set with plates and dishes, no table draped with a red velour cover. Before her was an alien display of the twentieth century. Here was a dish-washer, a food-mixer, a split-level cooker. There stood a washer with knobs and switches and dials, a rotary-iron, a waste-disposal unit. Clinically designed cupboards lined the walls, strip-lighting was strategically placed and carefully concealed. Everything glittered, but nowhere could Petra find anything in the way of comforting, old-fashioned food or drink.

The two rooms opposite the kitchen were blessedly in keeping and completely empty. They had, she supposed, been the domain of long-ago domestic staff. Now they stood forlorn with windows cold and bare and Victorian iron grates that were black and hollow as decaying teeth.

She closed her eyes and hugged herself tightly. Oh, old house, she yearned, I want to live in you, light fires in your hearths, warm you to life, again. I want – what *did* she want? A husband – Simon – to share it with her and two, maybe three children to play noisily in its echoing corridors and shout away the silence?

But images of Simon would not lend themselves to her fantasies and children with Simon's hair and eyes and smile refused to materialise at her bidding.

She was tired. Of course she was jumpy and fanciful. This day, and everything about it, had been larger than life. Today, for the first time, she had come to Wales, almost crashed her car, walked blindly through the mists to the edge of the still, cold water. Today, she had come to *Ty Mawr*, her inheritance, and met Gareth Davies ...

There remained the upper floor. Suddenly inexplicably wary, Petra walked upstairs to the gallery, clicking down each light-switch as she passed it. There were doors again to left and right, with narrow passages beyond, out of which smaller rooms opened. These were carpeted and panelled, with long, thick curtains that shut out the mist.

Apprehensively, Petra went from room to room. It was, she told herself firmly, only tiredness that made her fancy that if she turned her head suddenly she would see someone watching her. The atmosphere of the house was not unfriendly, but she was conscious of being a stranger here. Gareth Davies had made it clear that he considered her to be so, and now the watching silence pressed round her again.

A door at the end of the second passage resisted her touch. She rattled the knob, but the door remained firmly locked. There was no reason at all why her uncle should not have chosen to lock one of the rooms, but for all that, she felt a tingle of disquiet.

Perhaps the best thing to do would be to go to bed and explore further in the morning. No doubt Megan would have a key to the room. In the morning, in the sunlight, a locked door would present no problem ...

There were folded blankets in the cupboard and Petra took an armful and spread them on the bed. Suddenly she felt tired and the soft feather mattress beneath her prodding fingers felt irresistibly inviting. Just a quick check of the doors and lights, she thought drowsily, and in the morning it would all seem better. In the morning, she would get her car onto the road again, buy in some groceries, unpack her cases ... She sighed impatiently. She wished her cases were not still in the back of the stranded car. She had no nightdress, no toothbrush. She shrugged, unzipped her skirt and pulled off her sweater. Just for once, it wouldn't hurt her to sleep rough.

The room she had chosen, she reasoned, as she pulled the lavender-scented blankets close to her chin, was obviously the main bedroom, judging from the luxury of its furnishings. But there were no personal possessions in the wardrobes or drawers, and only the dark green of curtains and quilt hinted at masculine occupancy.

Reaching up, she turned out the light and instantly the walls of the room receded. Through the partly-drawn curtains glowed a rectangle of white mist and she closed her eyes tightly, shutting out the night, willing sleep to come.

There came instead a soft thud on the outside of the door. Petra jerked upright, her hand groping for the bedside lamp. The light made a comforting circle, banishing the darkness, casting a reassuring glow over the room.

She let go her indrawn breath, sliding her eyes back and forth, head immobile, neck rigid.

The soft thud came again and as she jerked her head towards the door, a child began to sing. High and sweet the voice echoed round the room ...

> *One, two, three Eleri,*
> *I saw Mother Carey,*
> *Waving wand for imp and fairy,*
> *Down in the valley ...*

Every word was clear and soulless as the peal of a bell, coming out of nowhere into the lamplit room.

Petra's mouth filled with the saliva of fear and beads of icy sweat broke out on her forehead. She sucked in her noisy breath as the last high note shivered into silence and into that silence cascaded ripples of laughter.

She sprang from the bed, her throat closing upon a scream. This wasn't happening! The house was empty and locked and she was quite alone. She had drifted into sleep and she had dreamed the noise outside and the childlike singing.

"This is ridiculous – *impossible* ..."

Her voice came roughly as, heart hammering, she crossed the room and flung wide the door with a noisy flourish.

Across the threshold rolled a bright red ball, bumping gently over the carpet, and in that instant Petra thought she had never before seen anything so frightening.

The passage outside the door was dim and silent. She

remembered the light-switch to her right and snapped it down but the sudden bright glare revealed nothing. There was no sound save that of her harsh, irregular breathing, yet someone – or something – had thrown the ball against her door. And a child had sung and laughed. She had neither dreamed nor imagined it.

In a sudden, overwhelming panic, she crashed the door shut then pulling up a chair, jammed it beneath the knob. Tears of fear were rolling down her cheeks now as she paced the room, eyes darting into each corner, ears strained. Once more she opened each cupboard door then slammed it shut again, the noise she made vaguely comforting. No one, nothing, was hidden there. She turned swiftly, expecting to see someone standing behind her, but she was alone. Fleetingly brave, she dropped to her knees and flung aside the bed-valance. Nothing, no-one, lurked there.

Stifling her sobs, Petra pulled a blanket from the bed and wrapping it around her shoulders, hugging it to her trembling limbs, lowered herself uneasily into the armchair. She was completely awake, now. She wished she were brave enough to open the door again but she was so utterly terrified that her legs were useless. But in the morning, in the daylight, she would find out who sang songs and played ball in a locked and empty house. And it had been such a silly little rhyme, hadn't it?

One, two, three, Eleri ...

Eleri? The name she had seen written in the book in Gareth Davies's bedroom? Surely Gareth Davies couldn't have ...? But he hadn't been pleased to see her. He had been downright hostile, in fact. Could he, she thought wildly, while she had been drying herself, have telephoned someone, warning them of her arrival? Or might he even

have had a key to the house himself? He had been very close
to Ifor Jones and it was reasonable to suppose he had. But
surely he wasn't the type of man to play such a cruel trick
on a woman alone in a big and empty house?

She tucked her toes beneath her and ran her tongue
round her dry lips, her eyes wide and watchful, determined
to stay awake at all costs, as she strained her ears for the
slightest sound.

But some time in the early morning hours she must have
drifted into frightened sleep, for sunlight, mingling with
electric glare awoke her. She jerked her head erect,
remembering what had happened. And it had happened.
The red ball lay in the middle of the carpet, still, and the
chair was where she had wedged it, to block shut the door.
Her body was stiff and cold and as she struggled to her feet
she caught sight of her reflection in the long mirror
opposite. Her face was pale, her eyes heavy and dark-ringed.
Her hair was tousled and all that remained of yesterday's
lipstick was a thin pink line around the edges of her lips. Oh,
what wouldn't she give for the sound of a voice, a flesh-and-
blood, human voice, offering her a cup of hot, sweet tea?

She sighed loudly, switched off the lights and cautiously
moved the chair from beneath the doorknob. At least, she
thought, it was morning. Through the tall, slim window at
the end of the passage outside, sunlight flooded
reassuringly, criss-crossing the carpet with long, angular
patterns. The bathroom, she remembered, was two doors
away, to her left. Swallowing loudly, she walked towards it.

Hot water gushed from the tap and she gasped with
delight. At least the plumbing wasn't hostile. A bath? Dare
she? Would the singing and the laughing start again if she
did?

Soft, pink towels and a bottle of bath oil coaxed her

gently. Of course it would be all right. You didn't hear voices in steam-filled bathrooms with a clear April sun shining through the windows.

She drew a deep, steadying breath, plugged the bath and turned on the taps. The bath oil was pungent with the smell of pine and its very masculinity reassured her. She dropped her blanket-wrap to the floor then plunged in an exploratory toe. The hot, silk-soft water caressed her cold limbs into relaxation. Slowly she leaned back and the water lapped about her chin. It was all right. The voices had gone.

Half an hour later, immeasurably refreshed, unbelievably brave again, Petra ran down the stairs into the hall and tugged open the front door. Cold, crisp air rushed in as she stepped outside and looked about her. The mist had vanished, save for long threads of gossamer that clung like fairy lace to the tree tops. From all around her came the singing of the river. She had not realised that it ran so close to the house and its winding beauty was nothing short of enchanting. She lifted her face to the sun. Beyond the rushing, willow-edged water, the mountains soared and gilded by sunlight, they seemed no longer to threaten or to warn.

Someone was cycling along the path towards her, someone blessedly plump with greying hair pinned back into a prim little knot, someone with a warm, wonderful voice and a hand that reached out in friendship.

"Miss Cunningham, isn't it? Well, that was a bad old beginning, last night! Nobody here to welcome you and not even a bottle of milk in the house! There's stupid, I told Gareth Davies this morning. Why he didn't bring you to my place, I don't know." She stopped, in need of breath, then smiled broadly, all the while shaking Petra's hand vigorously. "But I've brought along something for your breakfast, and Tommy will fetch the rest when he brings your car."

"Megan?" Petra smiled. "Megan Pritchard?"

She liked the look of the red-cheeked woman with the bright, dark eyes and softly hissing voice. Suddenly, everything around Petra seemed safe and normal again.

"That's right, *merchi*. Housekeeper to your mam's uncle since I was a girl," the other nodded, propping the cycle against the side of the house and delving into the saddle-bag. "Forty years I was with Ifor Jones."

"You don't look old enough," Petra gasped.

"Fifty-six next June," Megan nodded. "Now, would you like your breakfast in the kitchen? Warmer there it is. Were you cold, last night?"

"No. No, I was quite warm ..."

Petra followed the bustling little body across the hall and into the kitchen.

"Gave me quite a turn, this morning, when Gareth Davies told me you'd come," Megan continued, slipping a pinafore over her head. "All those weeks we've been expecting you and then you turn up without so much as a word. And you nearly got out of your depth in the dark water, by all accounts ..." She drew out a chair and motioned for Petra to sit at the table, all the while talking volubly. "Now, take my advice, and keep well away from that place. No good ever came from it – only heartbreak! Tea or coffee, then?"

"Coffee, please," Petra replied swiftly, "and what do you mean, *the dark water*?"

Megan Pritchard turned, a knife poised in mid-air. For a moment she stood completely silent then she pursed her lips into a little knot before saying quietly,

"You saw it, last night. The little lake in the dip below Gareth's place. Nothing much more than a glorified pond, I suppose, but it's deep and cold and dangerous. And nothing grows by it and no water-birds nest there. It hasn't got a name. Folks hereabouts just call it the dark water ..." She shrugged. "And a nice plate of hot toast, yes? Too thin you are, *cariad*, by far. A bit more flesh on your bones and you'd look quite bonny!"

She changed the subject so abruptly that Petra decided not to press it further, and besides, she had worries enough of her own without bothering herself with the sinister little lake.

"I am hungry," she admitted.

"That's right," Megan smiled. "The air here will give you an appetite. *Ty Mawr*'s quite high up, even though this is a valley."

"How far away is the village?"

"Oh, about two miles, up at the end of the valley. The main road runs into it, but between here and there, there's nothing but grazing land."

"Belonging to my uncle?"

"Most of the valley belonged to him," Megan nodded, breaking an egg into the pan. "Mind you, he allowed free grazing rights ..."

She shot an enquiring glance, her face eager.

"He didn't have any livestock of his own, then?"

"No. He made his money from the slate," Megan explained, "but the quarry is worked out, now. The good slate is all gone. Your uncle sold his share a long time ago and put the money into this house and the village. Built new cottages and rented them out very reasonable. A good man ..."

Again there came the hopefully enquiring look.

"I shall be going down to the village," Petra said, "when I get my car."

"Oh, and there's me hoping you'd wait until this evening," Megan protested, setting a plate of bacon and eggs on the table. "We're having a Noson Lawen for you."

"A nos – a *what*?"

"Noson Lawen." Megan said the words slowly. "A musical evening, to welcome you. Of course, it's all been got together in a hurry, but everyone would like to meet you, and I think you'll enjoy it."

"Why thank you! I'd love to come."

"Then let's hope the mist stays away. It's a nasty old thing. Comes down without any warning and goes just as quickly. But it makes things dangerous for people who don't know the valley, and for climbers, too. They don't realise how treacherous the mountains can be. Ah, well, I'll just put down a saucer for Moggy and – "

"Moggy?" Petra demanded, instantly alert. "Who's Moggy?"

"Your uncle's cat, Miss. When Old Ifor died, Moggy stayed here and wouldn't be tempted away. So I put out milk and food for him, every day."

"And does he play with a red ball?" Petra asked slowly, relief tingling through her.

"Yes, indeed. Have you seen him, then?"

"No, but in the middle of the night a ball bumped against the bedroom door. I looked about, but he wasn't there."

"Oh, the silly old thing hides under one of the beds when there are people about," Megan said. "But he might take to you, Miss, now that you're here. It must have given you a nasty shock, last night, and you thinking you were alone in the place!"

"Not really. I'm not a nervous person. Don't believe in ghosts, or anything ..."

"Well, there's nothing like that in this house," Megan retorted comfortably, pouring more coffee.

"Good." Petra spooned sugar into her cup thoughtfully, wondering why she was telling such stupid lies, wanting more than anything to tell Megan Pritchard about the singing and laughing and how very afraid she had been. "Are you having a cup of coffee yourself?"

"I'll have some tea later when I've cleared up, thank you all the same. Will you be using the big bedroom, Miss Cunningham?"

"No, I think perhaps one of the smaller ones." Standing up, Petra hesitated then said, "I noticed one of the upstairs rooms was locked. Do you have the key?"

"Key? Oh, it's bound to be somewhere around, Miss. Old Ifor kept the room locked for years. There's nothing much inside there now, I believe, except some old lumber. I'll have a look around for the key, though. And talking of keys, Tommy will need yours if he's to get your car back to you. And I'll give him some groceries to bring along. Normally, I'd stay and put your supper in the oven, but with the Noson Lawen tonight, you'll be well-fed in the village."

"What arrangements did you have with my uncle?" Petra asked. "I mean, regarding wages and hours?"

"I came every day when he was alive and he paid me two pounds a day. Since he died, I've been more of a caretaker, you might say, but I don't want paying for that. Now that you're here, Miss, I can carry on coming, if you'd like, at the old rate."

"We-l-l, I'm not rich, you know," Petra hesitated. "I'm not at all sure, yet, just what my uncle has left me ..."

"Well, you'll have the cottage rents for a start," Megan

pointed out. "Bill Jones Post Office has always been in charge of the rents. Been collecting them every week since Old Ifor died. But you'll see him tonight. You can talk to him then. It starts about eight, by the way, but Tommy will have your car back to you in good time."

Petra laid the car keys on the table, then half turned to catch a fleeting glimpse of a sleek, black shape darting behind her into the kitchen.

A wry smile flickered on her lips and then died. Oh, there was no denying it – the cat had rolled the ball against her door last night and for that small mercy she was grateful, but no cat had laughed that unearthly little laugh; nothing human had sung that haunting little rhyme.

One, two, three, Eleri ...

Despite the comfort of daybreak and sunlight and hot food, despite the reassurance of Megan's happy chatter, Petra shivered.

Just who was Eleri ...?

Three

Megan, having left cold chicken and salad in the fridge, departed at midday, pedalling expertly along the rutted driveway on her old black cycle. Already the house was perceptibly warmer with the heating turned on and the sunlight that danced across the river showed no signs of abating.

Shrugging into her coat, Petra closed the kitchen door behind her and turned her face gratefully to the Spring sunshine.

Strictly speaking, she supposed as she picked her way down a narrow, box-edged path, it was not a real garden at all, for the wall surrounding it had long ago crumbled and only traces of what must have been a vegetable plot remained. But late daffodils rioted along the riverbank and beneath the blossoming trees stretched a shimmer of budding bluebells. The air was so clear and fresh that it stung her nostrils and over the tops of the distant dark-green pines she could see the cottages of the village, clinging to the other side of the valley. Above them rose the mountains, their peaks shading one into the other, their tips still snow-covered.

And all this, she thought joyfully, was hers alone; the riversong, the mountains, the unbelievable peace, and she knew as she stood there that it would be impossible ever to tire of it.

She turned at the sounding of a horn. Her car was coming along the drive and she hurried over the tussocky grass to meet it.

"Miss Cunningham? I'm Tommy Pritchard, Megan's nephew."

A man with sleeves rolled above tattooed forearms climbed out, grinning at her out of a dark face very like that of the housekeeper.

"Did you have a lot of trouble getting the car free?" Petra asked as they shook hands cordially.

"No. No trouble, once we got a good tow rope. Gareth says you were frightened by a sheep."

"At least I didn't hit it," she said, tartly, noticing the other's knowing smile, wondering just how much he knew about the tension between herself and Gareth Davies.

But Tommy went on smiling and said tactfully,

"Auntie Megan has put a pile of shopping in the boot. Shall I take it through to the kitchen?"

"Please," Petra nodded, holding the door wider.

"I left the keys in the ignition," he said. "You'll be driving yourself to the Noson Lawen, will you? I filled up the tank, by the way."

"Of course, you own the garage! Gareth Davies told me. How much do I owe you?"

"Oh, settle up next time you're passing," he shrugged. "I'll get this lot into the house, shall I?"

He walked briskly ahead, arms straining under the weight of the heavy box, well familiar, it seemed to Petra, with *Ty Mawr*'s layout.

"I shall never use all this!" she protested.

"Well, Miss, we were hoping you would be staying," he

said, as if by way of explanation.

"But nothing is certain. My job is in London."

"I went to London, once," Tommy mused. "Oh, it was a great place, very bright and noisy. But after a day or two I was glad to get back to the valley and my own people."

"Don't you like strangers?" Petra asked, amused.

"I like the peace of the valley," he said slowly, "and I like having just enough work to keep me busy. It's not much use worrying about getting rich, hereabouts. It's not likely to happen, this side of Christmas!"

He gave her another cheerful handshake and tramped off.

"How will you get back?" Petra called after him.

"On my two feet," he shouted back. "See you tonight, Miss Cunningham."

When he had gone, Petra unpacked the groceries and ate the lunch that Megan Pritchard had left. The afternoon stretched ahead but she was feeling an unaccustomed tiredness which wasn't to be wondered at, she supposed, remembering the previous night.

In the small bedroom that Megan had made ready for her, Petra unpacked her cases and laid out her makeup and toilet things. It was strange to think that the entire house and all it contained was now hers. She had never dreamed that her mother's old uncle had lived in such a place, and lived here alone and unmarried, though it seemed that he had been loved and respected by his neighbours and tenants. Yet she scarcely knew anything about him. *Ty Mawr*, with its comfort, its bright lights and modernity, gave her no clue as to the character of Ifor Jones. When she had time, she must go through every drawer and cupboard, try to find something more personal that had belonged to

him. There was the locked room, too. It was surely strange
to keep a room locked for years without even letting one's
housekeeper in to clean it – unless, of course, Megan had
not told the truth.

Petra lay down and closed her eyes, letting the tiredness
flow through her. The sunshine that blazed through the
window made patterns on the carpet. It might have been
high summer instead of Spring. But she had seen the valley
in a different mood, she thought soberly. That was
something to remember if she were tempted to stay.

She reminded herself that it was not her decision alone.
There was Simon to be considered. If – *when* – they were
married, would he give up his London office and live here,
at *Ty Mawr*? Or would he, she wondered, expect her to sell her
inheritance and live the life of a suburban housewife?

But Ifor Jones had left the property to her, she thought
defensively. That in itself implied that he had expected
something of the great-niece he had never known.

She dozed a little, images moving shadow-like across her
mind, yet Simon, of whom she had been consciously
thinking, never came. Instead she saw Gareth Davies
running in slow, gliding movements along the bank of a
swiftly-flowing river, and on a bridge in the middle of the
river, Megan was bouncing a red ball and singing,

> *One, two, three, Eleri,*
> *I saw Mother Carey ...*

The dream was becoming a nightmare from which Petra
struggled to free herself, but her feet were stuck fast in
black, sticky mud and a black cat, big as a tiger, was
bearing down on her with snarling mouth. She was awake
at last, desperately thankful to be free of the strange,
distorted images. She had slept longer than she intended.
The sun had faded and she felt cold, though the room was
quite warm.

Switching on the light, she opened the wardrobe door and sorted through the few clothes she had brought with her, choosing a long, bright red tartan skirt and a black sweater. Simon had smiled patronisingly last time she wore the skirt, she remembered, saying it was quaint, or in other words, she supposed, downright old-fashioned. On the other hand, Petra thought, Gareth Davies would probably approve.

She sighed deeply. If he didn't, she wouldn't mind one bit and anyway, it was extremely unlikely that he would be there at all. She didn't know whether to be glad or sorry about it. In fact, she didn't know why she bothered to think about him at all. It could be, she admitted with absolute honesty, that she found his brusqueness, his obvious disinterest, to be something of a challenge. Perhaps if he had been more attentive, more normal, she would have dismissed him without another thought. And that, she decided, was exactly what she would do. After all, what was so special about the man? The set of his chin, perhaps, the deep, dark eyes? Or was it his great protective shoulders, his utter masculinity?

She laughed out loud at her stupidity. It didn't matter at all. She was going to marry Simon.

A little before eight, Petra locked the front door of *Ty Mawr* and drove up the track towards the lights of the village. It was dark, but not misty, and the moon was a lovers' moon, suspended among the stars that clustered round the dim peaks.

She was wearing the long kilt and dark sweater, her waist clinched with a wide, silver-buckled belt. Her hair winged loose over her temples and she had spent a long time doing her eyes, leaving her not entirely unpleased with her appearance.

The track along which she drove opened suddenly into a road which climbed steeply to the rim of the valley and the village beyond. The straggling main street was dimly lit by infrequent, old-fashioned lamps and the little houses seemed to be huddling together like gossiping old women, watching her.

As she reached the open square at the top of the street, Petra's headlamps picked up a little figure with waving arms. She slowed down, then stopped beside Megan Pritchard.

"Good evening, Miss Cunningham. I've been on the lookout for you. It's to Salem Hall you're to come, and everybody is waiting," she smiled.

"I'm looking forward to the evening very much," Petra replied, getting out of the car. "What is Salem Hall?"

"Oh, it's the chapel hall. We hold most things there – the Eisteddfod, and wedding breakfasts and funeral teas and jumble sales and Bingo. We make our own pleasure here, you know," she added, as if by way of explanation. "This way then, Miss."

They walked down the side of a large, dark building into a smaller one at the side. As they approached, light streamed from an open door and Tommy Pritchard hurried out to meet them.

"You found her then, Auntie! Nice to see you again, Miss Cunningham. Everyone is here and waiting."

They shepherded Petra into a large, crowded hall with long tables and benches down one side and a group of young people with guitars and drums arranging themselves on a dais at the far end.

"Quiet, then!" Tommy called, raising his hand. "Don't rush all at once, now. This is Miss Cunningham, from *Ty Mawr*, and very welcome she is, too!"

He turned and smiled at Petra and she was immediately engulfed in smiling faces and cordial handshakes and a murmur of quick, singsong voices that rose and fell like paths over the mountain.

"Lovely to meet you, Miss Cunningham. Better than London, isn't it?"

"You'll be wanting to learn Welsh?"

"Would you be church or chapel, now?"

"Lovely man, your uncle was ..."

"Give the girl a drink and let her catch her breath! You're making her dizzy!"

She was indeed feeling a little bemused. She had always heard the Welsh people were clannish and suspicious of strangers, but these villagers were falling over themselves to make her welcome.

"Miss Cunningham – I'm Bill-Post-Office."

A thin man with rimless spectacles took her hand in his.

"The gentleman who collects the rents," she remembered.

"Indeed, I have that honour – for a small commission. The money has been collected since Mr Ifor died, so there is three months owing to you. There are eight cottages down on *Ty Mawr* land and at five pounds a week, each, that makes a little more than five hundred pounds I've got for you."

"That sounds fine," Petra said, yet all the time wondering if the money aught not to be paid to her uncle's lawyers. "Look, could we have a chat, some time?"

"Indeed. Whenever it is convenient for you."

"At the Post Office?"

"The other side of the garage," he nodded. "You can't miss it. We do the Post Office business at the back and my sister runs the General Store at the front."

He turned, beaming, as Megan hurried up.

"There's supper ready, now, and a bit of a concert afterwards," she announced. "And you must meet our minister, Mr Gruffydd."

A short, cherubic man shook Petra's hand with amazing energy.

"And very happy I am to meet the great-niece of Mr Ifor Jones. I was a great friend of his, a very great friend. We miss him, you know. We miss him sadly ..."

Petra smiled, greatly touched, and allowed herself to be led to a seat at one of the tables.

The food was plentiful. There was roasted ham with leek sauce, pork pies, apple tart spiced with cinnamon and plate upon plate of cakes and jellies and trifles. And bara-brith, too, to remind her of Gareth Davies, who hadn't come.

She closed down her thoughts. She was welcome and wanted here and it gave her a feeling of contentment. And she was ravenously hungry, too, and allowed her plate to be filled to a level that in London would have been considered quite unacceptable.

Around her, talk swirled in a mixture of Welsh and English. The hissing syllables fascinated her, as did the ease with which they all switched from one tongue to another.

Their welcome had pleased her more than she could say. Even the news of her legacy paled beside this warmth that reached out and enfolded her, drawing her into its midst.

"We don't have much of an entertainment for you," Tommy Pritchard was apologising. "You have to go further afield for the big choirs, but my wife plays the harp very nicely. There are not so many of the young ones who'll learn the old instruments, now. Guitars, it is, these days ..."

They were clearing a space for a pleasantly-smiling woman in a flowered caftan who seated herself by a small harp, and, with no introduction beyond a shy nod of her head, rippled her fingers along the strings.

Silence fell as a melody whispered its way into the hall. The lights had been dimmed and only one spotlight circled the harpist who sat, head drooping, her long fingers caressing the instrument. The whispering notes began to sing and the song became a rhythm of earth and wind and water that flowed through them, linking them all in a shared longing for a beauty out of reach.

As the last sweet note hung quivering on the air, Petra realised she was gazing straight into eyes darker than her own; eyes that could mock and glitter with animosity. They held her in unflinching regard and she tilted her chin slightly and allowed a small smile to touch the corners of her mouth.

The lights went up again and the spell was broken. Gareth Davies walked across the room to her, nodded curtly and sat down at her side.

"So you're the guest of honour, Miss Cunningham?"

"Yes, but more for my uncle's sake than my own," she acknowledged.

"Oh, come now! You surely realise how much the natives enjoy paying homage to their liege lady!" he exclaimed, mockingly.

"I'm half native myself," she countered. "My roots are here."

"Your grandmother uprooted herself pretty quickly years ago!" he returned. "But now you suddenly find you belong here, just when you learn that you own the most part of the valley!"

"You have a wonderful way of making yourself

unpleasant," she said, her lips forcing a smile, her voice low with anger.

"Perhaps I see things more clearly than most."

"You know nothing about me," Petra snapped.

"Then you must tell me more, mustn't you? Come and dance."

He took her hand and pulled her into the space cleared for dancing and for an instant she was held so tightly against him that she could scarcely move. Then he released her abruptly and guided her into the dance with a grace unexpected in so heavily-built a man.

The music changed and the throbbing, primitive rhythm became a smooth waltz. Gareth's arm encircled her again and his hand clasped hers. She glided with him, their steps blending into a harmony that had no echo in their low-voiced conversation.

"If I step on your toes, Miss Cunningham, you must put it down to my peasant clumsiness."

"If you step on my toes, Mr Davies, I am very likely to jump on yours, very hard indeed!"

"Ah now, you are trying to prove to me that you are as Welsh as I am. Welsh women are supposed to have terrible tempers."

"And that is why you haven't married one of them, I suppose?"

His fingers tightened so hard upon her hand that Petra winced in pain.

"You have a sharp tongue," was all he said, but for an instant, Petra glimpsed searing, naked pain in the dark eyes above her.

"Only when I am attacked," she said, wondering what had caused that look.

"Then shall we cry a truce?" he said, levelly. "Did you sleep well?"

"Last night? Is there any reason why I shouldn't have done?"

"No reason at all, except that it's a big place and lonely, too, for one small city girl."

"It's a beautiful house," she said. "My great-uncle made it very comfortable, for all its size. I slept well."

"Old Ifor liked it. He seldom left the valley at all."

"What I can't understand," Petra confided, "is why, if he had kept track on me, he never invited me to stay, or anything. If he intended to leave everything to me, wouldn't you have thought he would have wanted to meet me?"

"He left *Ty Mawr* to you because you were his sister's grandchild, but he had no wish to meet you. He wasn't much for meeting people," Gareth Davies supplied, with an authority born of close friendship.

"Like yourself, I suppose?" The music had stopped and Petra looked up at him as he took her back to her seat. "You choose to bury yourself on a God-forsaken mountainside when you might be a success elsewhere."

"It depends what importance you attach to success. Tramping city streets with briefcase and brolly isn't my idea of success." His smile was wry. "I like the peace of the valleys and the hills. I'd not leave of my own accord."

"I'm beginning to understand what you mean," she admitted. "It is very beautiful, round here."

"It can also be harsh and damp in the autumn and often snowbound in the winter. We scrape a living from the slopes under the mountain and the fertile land along the river. There is nothing in the least romantic about delivering lambs when the tips of your fingers are frozen and your breath ices the air."

"But you wouldn't change it," she said, softly.

"No, because the mountains don't change. Oh, they have their moods, but they always remain where they are. They never move, never turn their backs, never pretend to be what they're not. There is an honesty in the land."

The music had begun to play again, but he was looking at her with a rueful expression.

"That truce between us might become permanent if you lead me on to talk about myself," he said, softly. "You'd better tell me something of your own life. You're not married, or engaged, I see."

"Not yet."

"But there's a man in tow, of course. Every city girl has a man ..."

"There is someone."

"And he wants to marry you, and you want to wait until he can support you in the style to which you are shortly to become accustomed."

"Is it really any of your business?" she flung coldly.

"Now Gareth, you mustn't keep Miss Cunningham all to yourself," Tommy Pritchard interrupted. "Would you like to dance, Miss?"

"Yes, please. Very much."

She tossed a tight little smile in Gareth Davies's direction and rose.

Tommy Pritchard did not dance like Gareth Davies. Tommy Pritchard danced as if he were driving one of his cars, steering her round with his hands on her waist, beaming every time they successfully negotiated a reverse turn.

"Your wife has great talent," Petra remarked.

"Thank you." He flushed with pleasure. "Mair likes to play, but she's a bit shy. She says crowds make her nervous. Are you settling into *Ty Mawr*?"

"Oh, yes. I've been poking around – exploring."

"Auntie Megan has always taken a pride in keeping it

nice. Goes on and on about the kitchen. A good woman, my Auntie Megan. Brought us up, after Mam died. Never married, herself. Never found the time, she always says."

"She worked so long for my great-uncle that I'm surprised he didn't leave her something in his Will," she ventured.

"Oh, she never looked for anything from him," Tommy supplied. "The property was to stay in the family. That was always understood, even when – "

He stopped, abruptly, his face uneasy.

"Even when *what*, Tommy?"

But her question went unanswered, for Bill Jones Post Office came up, smiling, as the music ended.

"Come over and meet my sister, Miss Cunningham. Myfi runs the shop I was telling you about."

"And it takes me more time trying to run my brother." Myfi, a trim, short woman, shook hands pleasantly.

"And everyone else in the village," Bill Jones Post Office supplied.

"And I suppose they call you Myfi General Store," Petra said brightly.

"Oh, no indeed. I'm called Myfi Chester," came the cheerful reply.

"Now, you'll never believe this," Myfi's brother said, his eyes dancing with suppressed laughter, "but Myfi went to Chester, once, on the back of Davy Williams's motor-bike. Or maybe I should say that she started out to get there, but they stopped off at Corwen for a cup of tea and Myfi went to the 'Ladies'. Well, out came Davy Williams, got on the bike, and roared away. He was nearly to Chester when he realised he'd forgotten Myfi!"

"He picked me up on the way back," Myfi laughed, "but

I never did get to see Chester. That's how I got the name, do you see?''

"I – I think so." Despite her bewilderment, Petra couldn't help responding to the other's infectious smile.

"Going to be a bit lonely," Myfi said, "up at *Ty Mawr* all on your own. Are you thinking of getting married, perhaps? That would be a lovely house to raise children in."

Her broad, dark face was full of friendly curiosity.

"I might just do that," Petra said lightly.

Over Myfi's shoulder she could see Gareth Davies approaching, and her heart gave a little leap of what she was sure was annoyance.

"Are you ready to risk another dance, Miss Cunningham?" he enquired.

"Later, perhaps – " Petra began, but his black brows rushed together in a frown.

"I'm only staying for one more dance," he said, curtly. "One of my heifers is due to calve down at any time, so I'll have to get back."

"Very well, then. Excuse me." Petra nodded pleasantly to Myfi and moved into Gareth's arms again.

The lights were low and the music soft. He held her closely and she surrendered herself to the melody, half-closing her eyes.

"You look as if you expected to be kissed," he said softly in her ear.

Petra's eyes flew open indignantly.

"I was enjoying the music," she said crossly, "and now you've spoiled it."

"By talking? So you like the strong, silent type? I suppose the man you're going to marry is like that?"

Was he? Her eyes opened even wider as she stared at him. It was strange, but she had not thought about Simon all evening. She tried to conjure up his face in her mind; the cool grey eyes, the thick fair hair, the sharp scent of after-shave that was as much a part of him as the plain gold watch and well-cut suit. But his face was dim as if she were trying to see it through a darkened window and she couldn't remember his voice at all.

"I wish you would go and – and see to your cow, or something," she managed at last. "You confuse me."

"It won't be for long," he replied. "When you've looked us over, you'll grow bored and go back to your streets and rush-hours."

"I'll not be pushed into any decision one way or the other," she jerked. "Not by you, not by the people in the village, not by anyone. I came here alone and I'll stay as long or as short a time as I choose!"

"And your man?"

"Is none of your business. And now, if you'll excuse me, I think I'll go home."

"You'll never get to a London train at this hour," he retorted.

"I meant home to *Ty Mawr*," she flashed. "Whatever prejudice you may have against me, Uncle Ifor *did* leave it to me, and I shall stay here! Goodnight, Mr Davies!"

She turned swiftly and left the hall, pausing in the alley as she heard Gareth Davies's voice behind her. His temper matching hers now, he said,

"If you think I give a damn whether you stay or go, you're mistaken. But I was Ifor's friend, and I know how much he cared about *Ty Mawr*, and the village. I can't endure to stand by and watch it all pass into the hands of a shallow young woman who can't even cross a meadow without getting her feet wet. And if I'm wrong, I'll be the first to apologise ..."

"And if you're right, then you'll doubtless turn

cartwheels all the way to the nearest Eisteddfod," she flung, almost running to the place at which she had left her car.

How dare he? How dare a perfect stranger presume to judge her character and her motives? What gave him the right to set himself up in opposition to the welcome all the others had given her? And why, oh why, had he danced only with her and held her so closely that Simon had become no more than a shadow in her mind?

She fumbled with her key in the lock, her breath coming in short, angry gasps, her fingers trembling.

Oh, how intensely she disliked Gareth Davies!

Four

Petra flung herself into the car and slammed the door hard, then winding down the window she leaned back in her seat, closing her eyes against her anger. Behind her, the sound of music still drifted through the open door of the chapel hall, and she realised, crossly, that she had left the party without saying goodnight or thanking the people of the village for their kindness. She sighed deeply, wanting to go back, yet unwilling to risk another brush with Gareth Davies. And what would she say? That she had just popped back to say goodbye, having left in such a flaming temper she had quite forgotten ...

No. She would see everyone tomorrow and thank them properly, when she was less angry, less confused.

Thoughtfully, she turned the key in the ignition and swinging the wheel hard over, headed back in the direction of *Ty Mawr*. Ahead of her, the road narrowed into the track which ran through the open pasture along the side of the river. She could see the moonlight sparkling on the rippling water, the trees gaunt and black beneath light, silver-tipped clouds. Gently she stopped the car and wound down the window, listening to the night-sounds, letting peace flow over her, ridding her of her anger.

The eerie screech of a hunting night-bird — was it an owl,

she wondered – made her wind shut the window and start the car again. Oh, if only Gareth Davies had been friendly instead of so hatefully mocking she might, Petra thought, have asked him back for coffee or a drink. It wasn't that she was afraid to be alone in *Ty Mawr*, she told herself firmly, but perhaps if Gareth had come back with her, his presence might have reassured her, a little. After all, the singing and the laughing had been a nasty experience. No one could blame her for being a little apprehensive about spending the night alone. Of course, she reasoned, if Simon had been able to come to Wales with her …

She felt a surge of remorse. She had no right at all to be thinking about Gareth Davies when she had not yet been in touch with Simon, although had there been a phone in *Ty Mawr*, things might have been different. Last night, for instance. What wouldn't she have given to have heard his voice?

She would write to him, she vowed, the very next morning, and ask him to come up to *Ty Mawr* as soon as he possibly could.

She was glad she had left the hall and staircase lights burning, and as she drew up before the front door, a shadow moved in the faintly illuminated window. Long-tailed and sleek, Moggy prowled the sill. And tonight he would be shut up in one of the bedrooms, Petra decided purposefully. There would be no more bouncing balls thudding against her bedroom door!

Another shadow, bigger than that of the cat, loomed ahead of her. Heart thumping, she flung round to see a bent old woman, walking slowly from the shadow of the trees.

"Who are you?" Petra gasped, her mouth suddenly dry. "What do you want?"

The woman lifted her head, the moonlight behind her casting her face into shadow. She mumbled something in Welsh then thrust a roughly-tied parcel into Petra's hands.

"For me?" Petra stared at it in surprise. "Is this for *me*?"

The woman nodded her head then turned and walked quickly towards the trees, fading into the darkness as if she had never been. Only the lapping of the water and the faint sighing of the wind in the trees companioned the silence.

Petra thrust her key into the lock, feeling relief as Moggy's soft warm body brushed against her legs, walking around her, tail erect.

The parcel was wrapped in brown paper and tied with pieces of string, knotted together to form one long, untidy length. Hardly able to stifle her curiosity, Petra went through to the kitchen and rummaged for a sharp knife. The ties parted easily, fraying at once, and the thick brown paper crackled open.

In her hands was a wooden doll, obviously hand-made and beautifully painted, dressed in the red cloak and lace-edged steeple-hat that Petra had come to associate with traditional Welsh costume.

Who the old woman was and why she should present this gift so mysteriously, so dramatically, Petra thought, were two questions more to be answered.

She laid the doll down and poured milk into a pan. The house was comfortably warm and there was a cheerful normality about the bright, modern kitchen that instantly raised her spirits. The door swung silently open as the large black cat walked in. Moggy had evidently decided to accept her and his grateful purring as she poured milk into a saucer added the final touch of domesticity.

She sipped her warm milk. Tomorrow, she would drive over to the village and find out just who the old woman was.

She would post a letter to Simon, settle her debts at the store and the garage and talk about the rents with Bill-Post-Office. Perhaps, if she could find a phone-box, she might even ring Simon's office.

She scooped up the brown paper wrappings and frayed string and pressing them into a ball, threw them into the bin. Something fluttered to the floor. Bending, she picked up a small piece of writing paper. It was old, and faintly yellowed around the edges and scrawled across it in a childish hand were the words,

I belong to Eleri.

Petra snatched at her breath, then repeated the words slowly, her lips wooden, her face taut.

"I belong to Eleri!"

The cat mewed, rubbing against her skirt. The doll smiled, its painted mouth pink under the tall hat. Somewhere beyond the window the night-bird cried again.

Petra threw down the paper as if it were white-hot in her hand and walked quickly to the door, snapping off the light. She had vowed that tonight nothing should make her afraid, yet her legs were shaking beneath her and as she climbed the stairs to the gallery, the darkness beyond the windows was menacing and hostile.

She stood for a moment, willing her heart to stop its pounding, taking long, deep breaths and all the while listening ...

This is *Ty Mawr*, she insisted silently. It is my house – my *home*, now. It is friendly and warm and Uncle Ifor intended that I should live in it and be happy. Tomorrow, I will ask Megan Pritchard about Eleri. Megan will know. There will be a simple explanation.

She straightened her shoulders and stuck out her chin.

"I am not afraid," she said, slowly.

Her words echoed loudly about her and served only to make her feel more alone than ever.

Megan had not arrived in the morning when Petra set off for the village. To her surprise and delight, she had slept deeply and the mirror showed her a fresh, clear-eyed reflection. It was odd how daylight diminished fear. She made coffee and fed Moggy who came out of one of the bedrooms, accepted her caress with feline indifference and took himself off through a low cat-door at the back of the pantry.

Petra rinsed her cup and went into the sitting-room. Before anything, she asserted firmly, a letter to Simon. She found it strangely difficult to frame the sentences as if something inside her denied the invitation she was extending. In the end she wrote briefly,

Dear Simon,

This is a most beautiful house, much bigger than I expected and the people are very friendly. I'd love you to come up at the weekend. Could you take Friday off and stay until Sunday – or Monday? If you can spare two days from the office I shall look forward to showing you around.

She hesitated and then finished with a flourishing capital P, and no other salutation.

Outside the air was sweet-scented and clear, the grass heavy with dew. Petra had put on a sweater and skirt of soft pink and was feeling her best. As she drove, she looked about for any sign of the old woman but the valley was deserted, except for a few sheep and several cows placidly grazing.

By day, the village revealed itself as a long, steep street with houses down both sides, flattening out at the top into a square, flanked by the chapel and chapel-hall and the double-fronted Post-Office.

Miss Cunningham, I've been hoping you'd come in," Myfi Chester called, hurrying towards her as she parked. "Tommy has taken his Auntie Megan over to Aberoer to the doctor's."

"Is she sick?"

"Well, she ricked her ankle last night as we were leaving the hall. Had her Sunday shoes on, see, and she's not used to high heels. I don't suppose you'd call it sick, but she can't put her foot to the ground. Will you be all right on your own? I dare say Tommy will be letting you know how things are, as soon as they get back."

"I shall be fine," Petra assured her. "I'll let Megan know she's not to worry."

"You were going to see Bill, I believe? He's gone up to the quarry. There's an old cottage up there – falling down, but the roof is still good. He's taking a few of the slates to do a repair job. Do you want to wait?"

"Well, I do have a letter to post," Petra conceded. "Could you let me have a stamp?"

"Indeed I could. And the kettle's on, so you'll be having a cup of tea while you're waiting?"

Petra nodded her thanks, following Myfi through to the back of the house to what was obviously the Post-Office section.

"First-class mail, is it?"

Myfi took the letter and squinted at it expertly but made no comment, lifting the flap of the counter to allow Petra to pass through into a small sitting-room at the back.

"Bill will be here before long, just as soon as I've wet the tea, you'll see!"

She bustled about, clearing newspapers from a chair to let Petra sit down.

The tea was strong and sweet and Myfi offered home-made shortbreads from a fat brown jar. Then she settled herself comfortably and looked expectantly at her visitor.

Petra stirred her tea, accepted a biscuit then said, ruefully,

"Look – about last night. I'm very sorry I went off as I did without saying goodnight or thanking anybody. You must think me – "

"Now, now, Miss Cunningham!" Myfi's eyes twinkled knowingly. "Just what do you think we all are, then? Spoil-sports, or something? Mind, I'll not deny that there were a few old-fashioned looks about the place when you left with Gareth, but it was nice to see him taking an interest again. Nobody minded, be sure of that!"

She smiled again and nodded.

"But Myfi ..."

"Ah, now, there's Bill. Didn't I tell you? The smell of tea ..."

She picked up her teacup, calling out something in Welsh.

"I'll be getting back to my counter, then, and leaving you to talk in private."

"Well now!" Bill-Post-Office held out his hand in greeting. "I have the rents ready for you, less my commission, of course. I hope the arrangement will suit. Ten percent, it is. Made it with Old Ifor a long time ago. Of course, if you'd rather make other arrangements ...?"

"No!" Petra returned, quickly. "No, I shall be happy to leave everything as it is," she assured him.

"Old Ifor used to see me once a month. He'd look over the books and I'd hand him the rents," Bill-Post said, rising to unlock a little wall-safe. "It's all here, safe and sound.

We can go through everything now while you have another cup of tea."

Petra concentrated dutifully on the lists of names and payments.

"It seems very straightforward to me," she said at last. "I'm very grateful indeed for all your help. Everyone is being so kind to me," she smiled.

"A privilege and a pleasure," Bill-Post beamed. "You'll be staying with us, then?"

"I have time off from my job," Petra told him. "It's not a very exciting one, working in an office, but there are other girls there. I share a flat with two of them."

"*Ty Mawr* must seem lovely and roomy, then, after such a cramped space," he said.

"It's a friendly house."

"You feel that? Ah, now, that's because you're a friendly person, Miss Cunningham. It will be even better there when you are married and the old place comes into its own again. Old Ifor never got wed, of course. A bit of a recluse he was in the last few years, but a real gentleman. Oh, dear me, yes."

"I'd better be on my way," Petra put down her cup and stood up to shake hands. "I hope you and your sister will come over to *Ty Mawr* one evening for supper when Megan is on her feet again."

As she went through to the front of the shop, nodding to Myfi on her way, the door was held open for her by a tall man with a thin face and sandy hair that rose in a crest from his narrow head.

She murmured her thanks and was surprised when he turned and fell into step beside her.

"Miss Cunningham, isn't it? Miss Petra Cunningham."

"Yes."

"I am Edward Bonner. I have been hoping to meet you."

"Oh?" She looked at him steadily.

"Your coming is not such a secret, you see. I understand you are here with the intention of selling *Ty Mawr*."

"Selling it? Who on earth told you that?"

"A young lady from London is not very likely to bury herself in a lonely old house in the middle of nowhere," Edward Bonner said.

"Surely that depends on the young lady?"

"Of course, of course. But I was under the impression that you'd come here simply to put the house on the market."

"I can't imagine where you got that idea," she said coldly, disliking his ingratiating smile.

"You'll excuse my putting myself forward in this manner, I know?" he said.

"Will I?" She raised her brows slightly.

"The point is this, Miss Cunningham. I know something of the extent of Ifor Jones's property, and I do know that it is not good land. The soil is thin and shallow and that river sometimes floods in very rainy weather. No point in trying to plant when the river is likely to wash the crops away."

"So?"

"So you'll see that it would make better sense to sell. Oh, I'm not saying you would get a fortune for it, but a bird in the hand – "

"Are you an estate agent?" Petra demanded, "Or are you making me an offer for *Ty Mawr*?"

"Oh, dear me, no! I'm not rich enough to buy your property on my own account."

"Then you're acting for somebody else?"

"I do admit to a certain interest in *Ty Mawr* on behalf of some friends of mine," he said, slowly. "Looking for a place for their retirement, you see, and they asked me to look around for something suitable. *Ty Mawr* would be ideal. They were in North Wales last year and chanced upon *Ty Mawr*. It wasn't for sale then, of course.''

''Nor is it now,'' Petra asserted firmly.

''Well, that's your decision, Miss Cunningham, but I do advise you to hear what the offer is first,'' he said, quickly.

They had reached her car and she bent to unlock it.

''As I said, the offer is a tentative one, but you might consider fifty-thousand pounds. That's for the house and land and cottages. My friends might be willing to go up a little, but they're not what you'd call rich.''

''Who are these friends?''

She slid into the driving seat and looked up at him suspiciously.

''Retired, as I said, and very reluctant to have their names made public at this stage. You might say that the gentleman in question did occupy a certain position in public life at one time, and is now anxious to retire as inconspicuously as possible. You'll understand that, I'm sure.''

''I suppose so.'' She started the engine, anxious to be away. ''But *Ty Mawr* isn't for sale, Mr Bonner, so I'm afraid your friends will have to look elsewhere for their retirement home.''

''Now you can't expect me to take that as a final answer,'' he smiled. ''A lady's privilege to change her mind, isn't it? I shall have a word with my friends, again, to see if they'll consider raising their offer and then I'll be in touch with you. Good-morning, Miss Cunningham.''

He was not wearing a hat, but he gave the impression of touching a non-existent brim before he walked away.

Shaking off the vague unease that the encounter had

stirred inside her, Petra drove back to *Ty Mawr*.

What next would happen, she wondered.

As she turned into the driveway, Petra saw a battered looking truck drawn up outside the front door of *Ty Mawr* and Gareth Davies, in thick sweater and shabby jeans, was leaning against the bonnet.

She parked her own car and got out with a face carefully controlled to hide the pleasure that was singing through her.

"I was up in the village," she said, "so you'd not have found me in. Have you been waiting long?"

"Only a few minutes."

"I have your wellingtons and your socks," she remembered. "I meant to return them, but if you'd like to come in I'll get them for you now."

"I didn't come for the wellingtons."

As she opened the front door he followed her into the hall.

"Oh?"

She glanced round, seeing him with his hands thrust deep into his pockets and his chin lowered.

"I came over to – apologise," he said, as reluctantly as if he were opening his mouth to have a tooth pulled. "I was out of line, talking to you as I did. That's my trouble. I'm apt to speak before I think, but the truth is I haven't got much time for city women."

Or any sort of women, Petra thought, but she kept the comment to herself.

"Anyway, I'm apt to be a bit hasty in my judgements," Gareth was saying, "Sorry, but it's the way I am made. Old Ifor was – well, I was fond of the old man. He had his funny ways, but he loved *Ty Mawr* and he cared, really cared, about the village and the people here. I didn't like to think of his home going to a stranger."

"And now?" Her glance was challenging.

"Now I'm apologising for jumping to conclusions. I can't say fairer than that, can I?"

"Apology accepted," Petra held out her hand. "We started off on the wrong foot, that's all. How would you like to stay and take pot-luck for lunch? Megan isn't here today."

"No. I heard about her ankle. They've been teasing her that she ought to take more water with it."

"Come into the sitting-room and I'll give you a drink, to fortify you before I expose you to my cooking," she invited. "There's whisky and sherry on the sideboard."

"Whisky, but only a small one. I don't want to stagger back to *Ty Goch*."

"*Ty Goch*?" Preceding him to the sitting-room she took two glasses and poured measures of sherry and whisky.

"It means the Red House. You wouldn't have noticed the other night, but the farm has red doors. Always has had, since my great-grandfather had the place."

"And if you decided to paint them green?"

"I wouldn't. I don't believe in flouting tradition," he grinned, accepting the drink.

Against the tanned skin of his face, his teeth were blunt and white.

"And you care about the village, too," Petra said softly.

"Too many villages in Wales are dying," he told her. "Either the youngsters move away to the towns, or the preservationists come in and try to make us all behave like stage Celts. We're expected to dress up and say 'Indeed to goodness', and spend our time singing hymns. Oh, that's a part of us too, but our heritage is richer than that."

"Do you always talk to women as if you were canvassing for votes?" she asked.

"With you, yes. I have to keep reminding myself that I saw you for the first time only two nights ago and that you represent the kind of life I would hate to lead."

"And if you stopped reminding yourself?"

"Then I would begin to talk nonsense," he said, brusquely. "I would tell you that a time comes when the beauty of the mountains no longer satisfies the hunger in a man. I would tell you that your eyes are the colour of the deep pool at Craig-y-Ben and that when you smile I understand how your grandmother must have looked as a girl and why old Ifor never forgot the little sister who ran away to be married."

"Perhaps we ought to have some lunch," she said uncertainly, putting down her untasted sherry. "I hope you like omelettes. I am rather good at them."

"If they're big ones. Do you want me to help you, or are you the sort of woman who likes to rush about being efficient?"

"I like someone to sit and talk to me," she said, promptly.

"Certainly. What shall I talk about? You haven't asked after the heifer yet."

"Oh, of course! Did she have her calf?"

"She did. Mother and baby doing well."

"I'm glad. Let's go through to the kitchen. You don't mind eating there, I hope?"

"It's the best place in the world to enjoy a meal. Moggy!" He clicked his fingers as the big cat strolled up.

"Moggy condescends to let me know that he's around," Petra said, as they went back to the opposite wing. "You know, I begin to feel a part of this place already."

She glanced back as they entered the kitchen, but Gareth Davies had stopped dead, the smile dying on his mouth, his eyes fixed on the table where the wooden doll was still propped.

"Where did you get that?" he ground, his face paper white, his eyes narrowed to a slit. "*Where did you get it?*"

Five

The brief peace between them was broken, the truce shattered.

"I meant to tell you about that," Petra spoke slowly, watching his face. "I forgot."

"You forgot. And do you expect me to believe that?" His voice was harsh, all friendliness gone. "Do you really expect me to believe that, when you've been up in the village all morning, gossiping, I shouldn't wonder? Who told you about it? Was it Myfi Chester? Did you get together over the teapot and did she tell you it was about time Gareth Davies snapped out of it? Was it like that, Miss Cunningham?"

"I don't know what you're talking about," she whispered. "I honestly don't know."

"I don't believe you!" He made no attempt to disguise the contempt in his voice.

"The doll was given to me – "

"It couldn't have been!"

"*Given to me* late last night. There was an old woman here when I got back from the village. She pushed a parcel into my hand. There was a piece of paper with it, saying the doll belonged to Eleri and that's the truth!"

"An old woman who spoke no English?" His voice became sharply questioning.

"She mumbled something I couldn't catch. Yes, it must have been in Welsh, I suppose. Then she just went — vanished into the dark …"

"She left the doll. I can't believe it. It was the one thing she wouldn't have parted with."

He whispered the words, reluctant to believe them.

"She?" Petra probed. "You mean Eleri?"

He nodded, dumbly.

"And the old woman?"

"Her name's Gwenny Carey. She's a bit simple in the head. Old Ifor used to call her Mother Carey."

Without thinking, Petra began to sing, the words coming more swiftly as she remembered them.

"*One, two, three, Eleri,*
I saw Mother Carey,
Waving wand for imp and — "

She broke off, her eyes widening, her voice trailing into a whisper as Gareth Davies lunged forward and gripped her by the shoulders, his iron-hard fingers causing her to start with pain. Between his clenched teeth he ground out,

"Those words! Gwenny Carey never told you those words!"

"No! No, I heard them!" She tore free from his grasp.

"Heard them! You *couldn't* have heard them!"

"But I did! The first evening I arrived — the night you brought me here — I heard that song. I heard it sung here, in this house. I don't know who sang it and I don't know where the voice came from, but *I heard it!* "

"And you said nothing? You were here alone and you said nothing! You expect me to believe that?"

"I don't give a damn what you believe!" Her voice was

trembling with anger and unshed tears. "I didn't say anything because I thought someone was trying to frighten me. I wasn't going to give anyone the satisfaction of knowing they'd succeeded. Was it Eleri who sang? *Was it?*"

"It couldn't have been." He stared at her, his eyes haunted. "No, not Eleri ..."

"Why not? Why couldn't it have been?"

"Because Eleri is dead," he ground. "She's been dead for ten years."

"*Dead?*"

"She drowned," he said, heavily. "She was drowned in the dark water below *Ty Coch*, ten years ago. The night before our wedding, if you must know."

"But the doll – "

"It was hers when she was a little girl. Mother Carey gave it to her when she was eight or nine, I think. Eleri must have given it back to her before – before she was drowned."

"But how could she have known to give it back? How could she have known what was going to happen?"

"She couldn't have, unless she had planned it – and I *know* she didn't plan it ..."

"But didn't anybody find out?"

"They tried. The verdict was 'Misadventure'," he said, dully. "I had to be satisfied with that. She set off to walk over to see me, it seems, but the mist came down suddenly. It wasn't like her to lose the way. She knew it well. She knew it so well. Oh, it's possible she lost her footing and panicked, but I've never accepted that, either. Yet why would she give Mother Carey the doll back?"

"Perhaps – ." Petra stopped, biting her lip.

"Perhaps she knew she was going to die? Isn't that what you're trying to say? That she gave the doll back and then walked into the lake? Eleri was a sweet, gentle girl, a chapel-going girl. She'd not have done such a thing! Not unless she was sick in her mind and Eleri wasn't sick."

"But why torment yourself now?" she whispered gently. "Ten years is a long time."

"To love one woman?" He shook his head slowly. "Not really."

"You thought I was Eleri," Petra said slowly. "You saw me at the edge of the water, in the mist, and you thought I was she."

"Only for an instant. Nothing more."

"Why, if she's dead?"

"I don't know!" he retorted, passionately. "Do you think that I haven't wished over and over again that she hadn't suddenly decided to come and see me that night? Do you think I haven't tried to forget her? And then *you* come! Do you realise how much you look like her? The same coloured hair, the same eyes, the same height ..."

"I'm sorry," Petra said, "truly I am, but *I'm* alive, Gareth Davies. Isn't it time to stop brooding over shadows?"

"Not until I learn the truth. Not until I find out how she got into the lake, *why* she drowned. I'm fit company for nobody until I find that out."

He turned abruptly and left the room and Petra heard his urgent steps echoing down the passage and the slamming of a door.

She stayed where she was, shocked into immobility, her eyes on the gay little doll. Such a pretty doll, given with love by an old lady to a little girl. But the little girl had grown up and given back the doll and been drowned on her wedding eve. And ever since then, Gareth Davies had wondered and worried. And when she had arrived at *Ty Mawr*, Petra realised, that old woman, thinking in her muddled mind that Eleri had returned, had brought back the doll. But could some part of Eleri have come back, too? And if not, then who sang her song at dead of night?

She sat down heavily at the table, saddened by Gareth's grief yet angry that after so long the wraith of a lost love could reach out from the shadow of the dark water to manipulate the present and hold back the future. Eleri was dead, yet her memory was alive in Gareth Davies' heart and for some reason, a part of her lived on at *Ty Mawr*.

Defiantly Petra clamped her lips together and stuck out her chin. *Ty Mawr* was *her* house, willed to her by Uncle Ifor and she knew instinctively that he had wanted her to live in it and be happy. For some inexplicable reason, she urged, she had sensed the singing, *sensed* it, surely, not *heard* it, and that was all. Whatever hold Eleri might still have over Gareth Davies is nothing to me, she thought fiercely. Let him live in the past, if that's what he wants. Why should I care?

But for all that, the dark, haunted face was before her as she ate her solitary meal and for the first time since their fiery meeting, Petra found pity in her heart for the tall, tempestuous Welshman with the black, brooding eyes.

Petra spent the remainder of the day going through every drawer and cupboard in the house, but her search yielded little. Obviously old Ifor's clothes had been disposed of – most likely to some worthwhile charity – but there were ivory-backed brushes and combs on the dressing-table in the main bedroom and a pile of letters in the desk. The letters, however, gave away nothing of his character. Many of them were simply notes about cattle sales and sheepdog trials and a rubber band held together a handful of Christmas cards, signed in Welsh. There was also a small photograph album. She looked through it eagerly but the pictures were blurred and faded and she could recognise none of the people in them. There was nothing else in the desk except a file of receipts and a ledger in which details of settled accounts and weekly payments to Megan were entered.

Petra sat down, running her fingers through her hair. Her great-uncle had obviously been liked by his tenants but had remained a private, rather lonely person.

The books lining the walls of the library were an odd assortment, ranging from bound copies of nineteenth century sermons to the latest paperback thrillers. There were cabinets filled with records and tapes, mainly of the classical variety, but nothing else to hint at Ifor's tastes.

Petra sighed and sat down in the button-backed chair by the fireside, her legs sprawling, listening to the quiet of the house, straining to hear the river-sounds and bird song through the closed windows.

What were you really like, Eleri? she wondered, realising that all through her search of her uncle's drawers and cabinets, Eleri's wraith had not been far from her thoughts. It was no use trying to forget her. She had to concede that whether she liked it or not, Eleri had become part of her life – the singing, the painted doll, and now Gareth Davies. She reached out from the dark water still, to torment and remind him. Eleri was dead, yet Eleri was everywhere.

Moggy mewed in the doorway then sidled towards Petra and rubbed himself against her leg.

"Good old Moggy," she whispered, stroking his funny, flat head, glad of his company. "Oh, what could you tell me, puss? Do cats hear singing in empty houses? Do they, eh?"

She jumped to her feet. She had done all she could, now. Only the locked room remained, its blank, defiant door a constant irritation. Every time she passed it, it nagged afresh at her. The whole house was so scrupulously tidy and clean that it seemed unbelievable that an entire room could be packed with rubbish and then locked up. Megan had said the key was mislaid, but Petra doubted that. It was more likely that she was still considered as something of a stranger and she knew with absolute certainty, that the locked room was not for strangers. She wondered if Gareth Davies knew anything about it. Gareth had once been a regular visitor to *Ty Mawr* – perhaps he might even be able to tell her where to find the key. But she suspected that it would be some time before she saw him again. Men such as he were proud. A man with troubled eyes whose wounds went deep didn't reveal them easily and having been forced to tell a little, was likely to retreat into silence again.

There was no sign, either, of Mother Carey. The old woman seemed to have come out of nowhere and vanished into nothing.

The doll still lay where Petra had laid it and suddenly she had a desire to be rid of it. It had belonged to Eleri and by rights it should be given to Gareth Davies. But he had looked at it with horror, with repulsion almost, and Petra knew it would be cruel even to offer it. Quickly she walked towards the kitchen. She would wrap up the doll and put it away. There was no need to be silly about it. It was only a toy – a little Welsh doll with a pointed hat and painted face and blank, unseeing eyes. Only a doll – Eleri's doll.

Petra snatched it up. She couldn't wait to place it back in its wrappings, to cover its face, to shut it away ...

After breakfast next morning, Petra drove up to the village. Apart from a skittish wind that whispered about the eaves and down the chimneys when darkness fell, the weather had shown a kindly face.

The deacon ambled eagerly towards her as she parked in the main square.

"Good-morning, Miss Cunningham. Very nice to see you again."

"Good-morning, Mr – Gruffydd, isn't it?" She hesitated over the pronunciation of his name.

"It is indeed. And how are you getting along, then? I hear you'll be having company this weekend?"

"You've been talking to Myfi Chester," Petra accused, smilingly.

"Ah, yes. A very chatty woman," he agreed, a decided twinkle in his eye.

"My friend is coming up from London, I hope."

"To see how he likes it, eh? Well, I wouldn't worry too much if I were you, my dear. Bound to feel the beauty of it, isn't he?" .

"Yes. Yes, of course." But she spoke with sudden uncertainty, her eyes downcast. Would Simon appreciate the rich heritage of the changing sky and the unchanging mountains, the warmth and kindliness of the people, or would he see only the cold, bare slate that lay tumbled against the wind-worried slopes?

"Going to see Megan Pritchard?" Mr Gruffydd was asking.

"Now how did you know that?"

"Because it is exactly what Old Ifor would have done," the deacon replied. "You are like him, I think, in many ways. A kind girl, I said to Mair, a very kind girl is Miss Cunningham. Is it true you are leaving the grazing rights free?"

"Yes, it is."

"Then I'm glad, for it means a lot, you know. Those

rights are in the hands of the owner of *Ty Mawr*, of course, but it's good pasture. I don't know of better, around here."

"But Mr Bonner said it was – "

"Edward Bonner? Have you been talking to Edward Bonner?"

"Yes. Outside the Post Office. Didn't Myfi tell you?"

"No, she didn't strangely enough." He drew his brows together, obviously puzzled. "But you didn't listen to what Bonner had to say, did you? Oh, he's not a man to be trusted. A man to be watched, Miss Cunningham."

"But he only passed the time of day with me," Petra supplied, evasively. Friendly as Mr Gruffydd was, she failed to see why she should tell him all her business.

"Well, I'll leave you to get on. Megan lives in that house there."

He pointed to a small cottage set back from the square, nodded pleasantly, and went briskly on his beaming way.

Petra rang the bell, and waited. There was a shuffling sound, then Megan opened the door, her face breaking into a smile.

"Well, there's nice, Miss Cunningham," she exclaimed. "Come in, do. I'm sorry I haven't been able to get over."

"It's all right. Tommy told me about your ankle."

Petra was shepherded through a narrow passage into a little parlour that was obviously only used on the most important occasions. The sofa was leather-covered and a framed picture of the Queen hung over the mantelpiece. In one corner stood a small piano, in the other a large aspidistra on a stand. Petra looked at it with interest, wondering if Megan knew that the plant so beloved of the Victorians was now enjoying a flush of expensive popularity again.

"Sit down and I'll make you some tea," Megan invited.

"Not with that ankle you won't! Let's go into the kitchen, and I'll make us both a cup," Petra suggested.

"Well, if you don't mind the kitchen, Miss Cunningham –"

"No, of course not. I like kitchens."

"In that case, then, come through, and welcome."

Megan hobbled ahead into a neat, warm room.

"The kettle is on," she said, lowering herself carefully into a flowered chair. "There's everything ready on the dresser there. It's really good of you to come over."

"I've brought you your money for the week," Petra laid an envelope on the table.

"But I haven't worked a week and it'll be Monday before I can come again," Megan protested.

"No reason why you should be out of pocket," Petra returned firmly. "It seems little enough for all the work you've put in at *Ty Mawr*."

"Ah, yes. Old Ifor said much the same thing many times," Megan nodded, gratified, "but I'd not take more from him and I'll not take more from you, if you'll not mind my speaking bluntly, Miss," she said. "Old Ifor was good to me and mine, more than you'll ever know, Miss Cunningham."

"I wish you would call me by my Christian name," Petra interrupted.

"All right – Miss Petra, then," Megan accepted a cup of tea. "I work at *Ty Mawr* as a pleasure, Miss. The money isn't all that important. This is my own house and Tommy is good to me, so I manage very nicely. Did you enjoy the *Noson Lawen* the other night?"

"Yes, I did. Very much."

"We saw you leaving with Gareth. Nice man, Gareth is, if you can get past his prickly outside. He's taken a bit of a liking to you, it seems."

"He was telling me about – about Eleri," Petra ventured, cautiously.

"About Eleri! Gareth told *you*!" Megan was clearly astonished. "Why, he's not spoken of Eleri for years, not even to Tommy and Tommy was her own brother!"

"Her own – " Petra put down her cup and spoke carefully. "Eleri was your niece, then – Tommy Pritchard's sister?"

"That's right. I brought them both up," Megan nodded. "My brother Ieuan, their father, was killed in the quarry and a few months later my sister-in-law died when Eleri was born. Tommy was about eight years old, then. Ifor Jones was very good to us. He saw Tommy through school and got him an apprenticeship with a big garage. And he stepped in with the money when the garage here was for sale. Tommy and Mair got married about the same time as your uncle put down the deposit."

"And Eleri was – drowned?"

"It was an accident," Megan whispered, her cheeks flushing scarlet. "She was going over to see Gareth, along the main road and across the meadow. She was like that was Eleri. Always taking it into her head to rush off and do something or go somewhere. Impulsive, she was. Latterly, I'd never know where she was. Anyway, she decided this night to go over and see Gareth but the mist came down and she lost her way. It was as simple as that."

"Gareth Davies doesn't seem to think so," Petra said. "He said she knew these hills. She wouldn't have been likely to walk into the water by accident or fall into it, or whatever was said at the time. Gareth doesn't believe that, yet he can't accept that she could have taken – ." She stopped, embarrassed.

"Gareth was always a deep one," Megan said slowly. "He's the moody type, Miss Petra, apt to go over and over things in his mind. Well, he would. He loved her, you see."

"Was she – was Eleri very pretty?" Petra asked diffidently.

"There's a picture of her – in the drawer, there." Megan pointed to the dresser. "It upsets Tommy still to see it, so I keep it put away. It was taken on her nineteenth birthday – the day she got engaged to Gareth."

The picture was wrapped in layers of tissue paper and framed in silver. Petra unwrapped it carefully then gazed at the head and shoulders of a young girl who had stared straight into the camera with a half-smile on her lips. Her long hair waved softly and her eyes held secrets.

"She was very pretty," Petra said at last.

"Very gentle she was," Megan said. "Very quiet and gentle. I never knew anyone so sweet-tempered. She was always over at *Ty Mawr*. Old Ifor thought a lot of Eleri. She used to amuse him with some of the things she said. They spoke English together and she made him laugh a lot when she was a little thing."

"And when she got engaged to Gareth?"

"She was very happy," Megan said firmly. "She didn't want a career, you know. She worked part-time in Tommy's garage and she did a lot at *Ty Mawr*, too. Oh, she was a good girl. Gareth couldn't have found a better wife. He worshipped the ground she walked on."

"Yes. Yes, I see." Petra's heart began to pound dully. If Eleri had been so perfect, then she was a formidable rival.

Rival? As the word entered Petra's mind, she rejected it. There was no reason at all to think of the dead Eleri as a rival because she was not in love with Gareth Davies. Loudly and cheerfully she said,

"My own boyfriend is probably coming on Friday. Just for the weekend."

"So Myfi was telling me," Megan began and looked faintly embarrassed.

"I guessed she might have told you," Petra smiled. "He'll be sleeping at *Ty Mawr*, too, so I'm wondering if everyone's going to be shocked ..."

"Oh, you mustn't take too much notice of what people say," Megan said. "We're a bit old-fashioned round here by London standards, but I don't think we're really any the worse for that."

"I know what you mean," Petra acknowledged, "I think I must be a bit old-fashioned myself ..."

"Then your young man will think all the more of you for it," Megan assured her comfortably. "But I can't help thinking that it's a pity you're answered for, in a manner of speaking. Gareth Davies is a fine man and these past ten years have been lonely for him. We all know that, though nobody says anything."

Petra's heart began to thump again. She wished Megan wasn't quite so frank in her observations. I wonder, she thought, just what everybody made of the *Noson Lawen*. We danced together quite a lot, Gareth and I, and left together ...

"I really came to ask you for the key to the locked room," Petra said, shaking all thoughts of Gareth Davies out of her head, deftly changing the course of the conversation. "You do have it, don't you, Megan?"

It was a shot in the dark, and for a while there was a silence in the little room. Then Megan slowly nodded her head.

"Yes, I've got it. Old Ifor left it with me," she acknowledged. "When he was taken ill, he gave me the key and told me to do whatever I pleased with the stuff inside. I didn't know rightly what to do, so I put off doing anything.

You see, I wanted to meet you, Miss; find out what sort of a person you were."

"And now that we have met?"

Petra spoke lightly but she felt a strong desire to be accepted by this kindly-faced woman.

Megan gave her another long look, then slowly drew a key from the handbag at her side and put it into Petra's hand.

"You're Ifor's blood-kin," she said, simply. "You'll do what you think best."

"You'll be back soon?" Petra asked, rising.

"By Monday I'll be fine," Megan promised, "but how will you manage over the weekend with all the cooking to do?"

"We'll probably eat out, but I can cook quite well, you know, Megan."

"I'm sure you can, Miss."

"I'll be on my way then. Don't get up. I can let myself out," Petra assured her.

"Nice of you to have come," Megan whispered as Petra left, "and I'm glad we had our little chat."

Her voice was low as she said it and her eyes were sad, and far-away.

Petra called at the shop, agreed with Myfi that it was so warm one might mistake it for a summer morning then walked back to her car. She had half-hoped that she might see Gareth, but there was no sign of him. Only the sunlit square with the dark bulk of the chapel met her gaze. After a moment or two she got back into her car, wondering what Myfi Chester, who had become very busy cleaning the plate-glass window of the store, made of her hesitation. Impatiently she switched on the ignition and pushed the car into gear. There were more important things to think about now. In her pocket was the key to the locked room ...

Petra closed her fingers around it and felt a shiver of apprehension tingle through her, for it was unbelievably icy to her touch.

Six

When she reached *Ty Mawr*, Petra went at once to the upstairs wing and the room that stood enigmatically defiant. For one agitated moment she wanted to turn away from the blank, tormenting door, drop the key into her pocket and run downstairs to the safe sanity of the twentieth century kitchen. But she stood her ground, mouth dry, jaws clamped, and with a mixture of apprehension and excitement, fitted the key into the brassbound lock.

Slowly she pushed open the door, the tip of her tongue encircling her dry lips. There was no creaking of hinges, no cobwebs to brush her face. What she had expected to find, she had never been quite sure, but the room, like the other upstairs apartments, was furnished as a bedroom, with a thick, fitted carpet and long, rose-sprigged curtains that matched the quilt on the brassbound bed. And there its conformity ceased, for the briefest of glances told her beyond any doubt that everything in that room could have belonged to no one else but Eleri Pritchard.

On the shelves were books, mainly school-stories and Victorian classics, with the name Eleri Pritchard written on their flyleaves in a round, childish hand. On a desk set crosswise in a corner, was a jigsaw with the pieces still fitted together, and a large paintbox with half the paints dried up and the brushes chewed and flattened at the end.

Petra drew in a steadying breath, closing her eyes against the mental picture that arose so vividly in her mind. Before her sat a child, bending over with a frown of concentration between her brows and a paint brush between her teeth. She shook her head, willing that picture to go away, wishing her heart was not beating so madly.

She opened the large wardrobe. Hung in plastic bags were coats and dresses, some of them belonging to Eleri's childhood, faded jeans and a pile of thick-rib sweaters, cotton dresses in pretty floral patterns.

There were magazines, yellowed round the edges with recipes ringed in red crayon, a piece of half-finished embroidery and a small silver cup, proclaiming that Eleri Pritchard had won it for recitation in the school Eisteddfod. There was a scrap-book with postcards pasted in it.

Petra shivered in spite of the warmth of the morning for it seemed that she was looking at the record of a brief and tragic life. From everything about her, she could build up a picture of Eleri. A quiet, rather old-fashioned girl who wore her clothes with care, who liked reading and cooking and was sentimental enough to keep her old games and jigsaws. Here, in this shrine to Eleri, there was nothing to explain the secret smile on the face of the nineteen-year-old girl in the silver-framed photograph. Certainly there was nothing that might remotely suggest she might have taken her own life. Surely Gareth Davies had been wrong? Hadn't it been a freakish, tragic accident?

Shrugging, Petra opened the smaller of the two wardrobes and there, shimmering faintly through its cover, hung a long, white dress. She lifted it out and unwrapped it carefully. This was the gown Eleri would have worn on her wedding day. Of ivory satin with a high-necked yoke, long, tight sleeves and full skirt, it was a romantic dress. On the shelf above, a veil floated from a circle of orange-blossom.

Seized by an impulse she could not control, Petra reached up for the bridal-wreath, disturbing as she did so, a little cloud of dust.

The circlet of blossom fitted snugly on her forehead; the veil floated like gossamer around her shoulders. Slowly, head erect, she walked over to the long mirror that stood between the windows and standing before it, gazed at her reflection, trying to picture Simon at her side.

"We can get married any time you say the word," he had said. "You don't want a fuss, eh, darling? Just a quick trip to the Registrar's ..."

But she didn't want a quick trip to a Registrar's office. She wanted to walk up the aisle of a church in a long, white gown, with an organ playing and the man she loved waiting for her with the look in his eyes telling her she was the most beautiful thing he ever saw. But she could not, no matter how hard she tried, fit Simon into the picture. Instead, she could only imagine a tall, broad-shouldered figure with black hair curling over his forehead. And that made no sense at all, because she had not the slightest intention of allowing herself to fall in love with Gareth Davies. Not ever.

Something unseen shattered her thoughts and instinct spun her round to face the window to her right. From the rough track below a bent figure was gazing upwards.

"Mother Carey!"

Petra backed away from view, her fingers fumbling clumsily with the blossoms that had become entangled in her hair. Gently as her impatient hands would allow, she laid the circlet on the bed and as she ran down the stairs, she rehearsed what she would say to the old woman.

"Please don't be afraid? Eleri hasn't come back. It was only me you saw, trying on her wedding veil. You gave me the doll because you thought I was Eleri, didn't you? But why did she give that doll back to you? Did she want you to have it as a souvenir of her childhood or did she know she was going to die?"

But it was useless, Petra fretted, as she flung open the front door. The old woman spoke no English; how then could they communicate? How would she ever learn the truth about Eleri?

"Wait," she called, running down the steps and onto the gravel path. "Oh, please, *please* wait?"

But nothing moved on the track beyond or in the trees that sloped down to the riverbank. Mother Carey was gone, but on the step at Petra's feet lay a flat paper parcel. Gently she picked it up, took another look around, then closed the door. On the kitchen table she pulled off the brown wrapping paper.

There were four pictures, painted on sheets of white cardboard, and that was all. Carefully, she turned them over, looking for a pencilled message or a scrap of paper, but there was nothing. Laying them side by side on the table, she studied them carefully.

The pictures were roughly drawn, crudely and brightly coloured. Three of them were of flowers – roses, daffodils, tulips and buttercups jumbled together in vivid confusion. The pictures, primitive as they were, sang with the joy of living.

The fourth picture was different. There were no flowers now, only an expanse of water under a storm-ravaged sky and in that sky an eye, red-pupilled and baleful. Watching.

Petra sat down and stared at the paintings. That Eleri had created them was beyond doubt, for her name was written in black across the corner of each one. On the flower pictures, it was written in the round, childish hand she had seen in the books, whilst on the fourth, the signature was uneven and slanted shakily backwards, as if the writer had been under an intolerable strain. So, no matter what conclusion she had arrived at only a few minutes ago, it was once again feasible that Eleri could have killed herself – the unhappy picture with its sinister eye glaring down over the dark water made that all too clear.

But how had it happened, and why had it happened? What had changed a joyful girl into the one who had seen no help or hope save in the shadows of the lake?

Carefully Petra folded the paper around the pictures again, then taking the doll from the desk, carried them back to the room upstairs. Eleri's doll and Eleri's pictures should, by rights, go in the room that once, surely, must have been hers.

Sadly Petra took the white dress, and wrapping it round with its plastic covering, hung it back in the wardrobe. How fond of Eleri must old Ifor have been, mused Petra, that he should have left untouched for so long, the room that once she used.

Had she played in that room, claimed it as her own, or had she lived at *Ty Mawr*, a substitute for a little sister who had run away to marry and whom Ifor Jones had been too proud to contact? How awful it must have been for the old man, Petra thought, to learn of her death on the eve of her marriage to his neighbour and friend. Had old Ifor suspected, as Gareth obviously did, that Eleri's death had not been an accident, and if this was so, why had they accepted the verdict of 'Misadventure' that had been returned?

Taking a last look round, locking the door again, Petra sighed. There had been nothing sinister in the room that might cause her fear or distress. She felt only a lingering sadness for a young life cut short and of hope wasted in the dark waters of a lonely lake. But for all that, an eye watched her as she slipped the strangely-cold key into her pocket, and a restlessness that would not be defined followed her downstairs where Moggy waited hungrily.

It sometimes seemed to Petra as the week went by that she had lived in the valley all her life. *Ty Mawr* enfolded her with its comfort and gentleness and all about her was the changing beauty of the mountains.

She explored the valley and the riverside on foot, enjoying the feel of grass beneath her feet and the sparkling clarity of the air. Scrambling up to the narrow road that joined *Ty Mawr* land to the next valley, she was able to look down to the still, dark lake and the farm where Gareth Davies lived. Smoke was rising from its squat chimney, but there was no other sign of life. Yet in her own mind, she was certain that Gareth was at home and wondered at the sudden impulse of shyness that held her back from walking nearer.

She tried, without success, to discover where Mother Carey lived. Even Myfi, who knew almost everything, wasn't certain, when Petra enquired.

"We-e-ll'– she used to sleep in an old cottage, half way up *Craig-y-Don*, but sometimes she wanders off for weeks at a time. She was always a bit odd, but she's gone downright peculiar these last few years. Mind, she doesn't do anybody any harm," she added comfortably, "so we leave her be."

"I was interested in talking to her," Petra said, dubiously, hoping Myfi wouldn't become too interested in her quest for the old woman.

"Well, now, you'll find that a bit difficult, Miss." Myfi quirked an enquiring eyebrow. "Mother Carey only speaks Welsh."

"I shall have to take lessons," Petra smiled, stepping gratefully onto safer ground.

"Indeed you will. There'll be a class over at Aberoer in the autumn. By next year, you'll be chatting away – "

They took it for granted, Petra thought, that she would be staying. Indeed, she had written to her flat-mates, enclosing her share of the month's rent, and enthusing over her valley so much that, on re-reading the letter, she was certain that Iris and Penny would not be expecting her to return.

There remained Simon to convince. She was reluctant to admit to herself that he might be bored by the quietness. Simon liked speed and gaiety and the bustle of crowds. Yet surely, with his flair for colour and design he would appreciate the contrast between snow-clad peaks and flower-filled valley. Even the slate that lay like the abandoned bricks of some primaeval giant across the landscape had a harsh, earthy quality that appealed to something fierce and unyielding in her own nature. Gareth Davies was like the slate, his personality subtly coloured, his edges sharp.

"Was there anything else you wanted?" Myfi was asking.

"No, thank you."

Hastily Petra captured her wandering thoughts and brought them firmly back to reality.

"I'm going to look in on Megan."

There were questions to be asked that would wait no longer, questions about Eleri and the locked room at *Ty Mawr*.

"Ah, now. She's not in. Tommy's taken her over to the

doctor, but I've heard her ankle is going on nicely," Myfi
supplied.

"In that case, I'll be on my way, then."

It would wait, Petra decided. When Megan was good
and ready, she would explain.

"'Bye, Myfi," she called.

She was driving towards *Ty Mawr* when she saw the
other car ahead of her. It was being driven too fast along the
track. A sheep, bleating indignantly, jumped from its path.
As she drew up in front of the house, Edward Bonner
alighted from his own car.

"Miss Cunningham! Glad to find you in!"

"I'm not in," she said coldly.

"Just arrived back, then? Surely you can spare me a few
minutes of your time?"

"Not if you're still trying to buy *Ty Mawr* for those
evasive friends of yours."

"I did promise that I'd approach you once more on their
behalf ..."

"And I told you that I didn't intend to sell."

"Then at least let me help you with your shopping?" He
took the bag from Petra's hands with a masterful air.

"You can come in for a few minutes," she said
reluctantly. "I'll make you some coffee."

"Now that's very kind of you, Miss Cunningham." He
had begun to follow her towards the kitchen, but she took
the shopping from him and ushered him into the sitting-
room.

"I see you've kept it as your uncle had it," he
commented.

"You've been here before?" Petra looked at him in
surprise.

"Once or twice. Your uncle was not, of course, intending

to sell the property then, though I'll admit that I did hint at the possibility. But he told me that when he died the estate would go to a distant relative. I imagine he expected it would be sold after he died."

Petra made no comment.

"If you'll wait here, I'll bring some coffee," she retorted sharply, wondering why the man irritated her so.

In the kitchen she put down milk for Moggy and waited for the kettle to boil. When she returned to the sitting-room, Edward Bonner was gazing through the window.

"The garden is all gone to seed," he commented, turning abruptly as she came in. "Not that Ifor Jones ever bothered with it very much. A bit of a recluse, he was."

"Like your friends?" Petra retorted, sweetly.

"Ah, but they are charming people. His work, now – I really shouldn't say this, but I'm sure I can rely on your discretion – his work was, at one time, of considerable national importance. Now that gentleman wants the peace and quiet of country life."

"And relies upon you to choose a house for him?"

"I'm flattered by his confidence in me," Bonner retorted smoothly, letting Petra's sarcasm flow over him unheeded. "Two lumps, please."

"You don't live round these parts?" Petra handed him the coffee cup and took a chair.

"I was born here," he shrugged, "in the village, but I had more sense than to stay. There's no future for places like these. No, as soon as possible, I went to London, feeling my feet, doing this and that, you might say; a stint in a factory, a bit of experience in the used-car business. I even worked in a theatrical agency for a time. Now and then I come back here, of course, but I've no family living and I find the people in the valley very narrow. A bit envious of a self-made man, I suppose they are."

"They've been very friendly to me," Petra jerked bluntly, disliking him more than ever.

"Ah, but then, you are Old Ifor's niece. There's a lot of the old tip-my-hat-to-the-Squire mentality still in these parts. Heady stuff, at first, but you'll soon get bored with it."

"You'll have to allow me to be the best judge of that," Petra retorted crisply, rising to her feet, wondering what could have possessed her to ask the man in at all. "Now, if you'll excuse me, I have a great deal to do."

"I am empowered to offer you sixty thousand pounds," Edward Bonner said abruptly. "My friends are not prepared to go higher than that. Sixty thousand is their final offer. After all, the land is scarcely worth anything and the cottages are very small, and tenanted. I'll grant you that *Ty Mawr* itself is a fine house, but – "

"I have absolutely no intention of selling," Petra ground.

"Then you're making a mistake, Miss Cunningham, a very great mistake. Now why don't you let me write out a cheque as a token of good faith? It won't bind you to anything?"

"Will you please leave?" She walked through to the hall and opened the door.

"It won't do you any good to hold out for more," Bonner said. "Nobody round these parts has the sort of money my friends are offering."

"The matter doesn't arise. I am just not interested." She clipped off each word, her eyes stony.

"I still hope you'll change your mind," he said softly as he left.

Petra drew in an angry breath. She was strongly tempted to slam the door shut after him, but she stayed where she was until the car, sleek and polished as its owner, had driven away.

This, she thought angrily, was a foolish situation. Edward Bonner had no right to badger her in this way. She was becoming more and more determined to stay on in the village and if that was what she intended to do, she reasoned, then it was only commonsense to be on good terms with her neighbours.

She hesitated for a moment, then hurried back into the house, collected handbag and wellington boots and walked determinedly to her car.

As she drove up the high ridge road she kept her mind firmly on the twists and turns of the way ahead. What she would say when she reached *Ty Coch*, she had no idea at all. She only knew she was being foolish, for as sure as night follows day, she was aware that somehow she would manage to end up by quarrelling bitterly with Gareth Davies as she usually did. But there was something fascinating about those dark, secretive eyes, something about the set of his arrogant shoulders that intrigued her, made her want to know him better.

She clucked impatiently. What on earth was she thinking about? So much fuss and bother, so much soul-searching, and all she intended to do was to give back one pair of battered old wellingtons.

She was making quite a production out of it, wasn't she?

Seven

Smoke still spiralled from the chimney as Petra drove through the open gate into the cobbled yard at *Ty Coch*. There was a furious barking as the sheepdog sensed the approach of a stranger.

"*Bedi matter*, Gyp?" Gareth Davies came around the side of the house and stopped, his face hardening.

"Good afternoon. Is it safe for me to get out?" Petra smiled.

"Gyp won't hurt you." He snapped his fingers at the animal who dropped to its haunches, panting. "A barking dog never harmed anyone. It's when they show their teeth you need to watch out. Remember that."

She nodded, chastened, determined not to provoke him to anger. Then clearing her throat noisily she hesitated,

"You didn't take your boots back. I've got them here ..."

She scrambled out of the car and offered them to him.

"You shouldn't have troubled. I wasn't in need of them."

"Oh, well ..." She flushed under his mocking scrutiny.

"Have you had your tea?" he demanded, suddenly.

"No. No, I haven't ..."

"I've just made mine. There's enough for both of us."

It was not the most gracious of invitations, Petra reflected, wryly, but for all that, she followed him into the long, low-ceilinged room. The smell of frying bacon and sausages met her.

"I'll get an extra plate," he said. "Can you cut decent slices of bread?"

"I'm not helpless." Tongue in cheek, she picked up the knife.

"I'm not very hungry, really," she said when eventually they faced each other across the table. "I've not long had a cup of coffee with Edward Bonner and he's quite taken away my appetite."

"I suppose he told you he wants to buy the house?"

"As a matter of fact, he did," Petra gasped, surprised at the calmness with which he imparted what she had supposed to be something of a confidential matter. "Just between you and me, he offered me sixty-thousand pounds for it."

"That's a lot of money in these parts." Gareth chewed bacon thoughtfully.

"It's a lot of money to me, too."

"So you'll sell out," he said, flatly. "You'll grab the sixty-thousand and hot-foot it back to London with the money burning holes in your pinny pocket. I thought your new-found roots went deeper than that!"

"Will you stop it! Will you just *stop* it and listen to me!" Petra demanded. "I told you that I wanted to stay here at *Ty Mawr*. Oh, when I first arrived, I wasn't quite sure, but everyone has been so welcoming and the place is so beautiful, I think I made up my mind a long time ago. I wouldn't do business with Edward Bonner, anyway. There's something about him that I don't like. I'm going to stay here, so if we are going to be neighbours, we might as well be friendly ones."

"I wasn't very friendly last time we met," he said,

eventually, his eyes downcast. "To tell the truth, I'm a bad-
tempered type, inclined to brood a bit, I'm afraid, and
seeing that doll on top of everything else gave me a bit of a
jolt. She loved that old doll."

"Eleri?"

"Eleri." He spoke the name softly. "She really loved it.
Oh, she had other things, I suppose, but that doll was a
kind of talisman. She used sometimes to carry it around
with her, even to talk to it. After – after she died, that was
the one thing we couldn't find. I always had the idea it was
still at the bottom of the lake. I never thought she might
have given it back to the old woman."

"And she gave it back because she knew she was going to
die?" Petra whispered.

"It would confirm what I've sometimes been forced to
think," he said, pushing aside his plate. "Oh, I know the
verdict was 'Misadventure' – I *want* to believe that – but
there's something that isn't quite right about the whole
thing. Something that doesn't fit that verdict, if I'm to be
honest with myself."

"Then you must have a reason, Gareth?"

"No. No reasons. No proof of anything at all," he said,
slowly. "I'd accept it – really I would – but for one thing.
I've never told anyone this and I don't have any concrete
reason for saying it, but I knew Eleri. I knew her all her life.
She was an old-fashioned kind of girl, very sweet-tempered,
not ambitious or hard. And she was contented here,
until – "

"Until what?"

"Until a few months before the wedding," Gareth jerked.
"There wasn't anything I could put into words, nothing I
could question her on. But sometimes she would fall silent
when we were together and then she would start chattering

about anything that came into her head. But there was an empty look at the back of her eyes. I put it down at first to the fact that she was nervous about getting married. She was shy, you see, and Megan had brought her up very strictly. I respected that. I really respected that and I wanted to make her happy, to cherish her ..."

"Then she was very lucky," Petra said, soberly.

"Oh, it sometimes all gets beyond me," he said softly, "and anyway, I used to think it was me was the lucky one. But perhaps I was wrong. Perhaps she was one of those rare souls who are not cut out for marriage. I don't know. I don't know anything any longer."

"Maybe you've thought about it for such a long time that it isn't so clear to you," Petra suggested.

"Perhaps. I only know that for ten years I have thought about it, wondered what made her so unhappy. And then the doll turned up and I knew I couldn't fool myself any longer."

"She might have given the doll back to Mother Carey because she was going to be married," Petra suggested.

"Dear Lord! If I could only believe that!"

"She could have lost her way in the mist – tripped and fallen?"

There was no real conviction in Petra's voice, for it was impossible to forget that crude painting of the lake and the eye glaring down from the storm-tossed sky.

"It may be so." He rose, lifting his shoulders as if he were shrugging off a burden.

"You haven't finished your tea," Petra remarked flatly.

"Neither have you. I hope I haven't caused you to lose your appetite, too."

"No. I've eaten so well since I came here – too well, in fact," she smiled, matching his suddenly changed mood.

"It must be the air, or something."

"And are you sleeping well? You haven't heard – "

"I've heard nothing," she said firmly. "In fact, I'm beginning to think it must have been my imagination. Perhaps I fell asleep and dreamed without knowing I had done so."

"Then let's not talk about it any more." He held out his hand. "I'll show you the rest of the farm, if you like. I've a couple of hundred acres where I graze my sheep and there's four fields that I put down to fodder. It's mostly stony ground, but the animals seem to know the right places to go. Sheep are not as stupid as some folk would have us believe."

He whistled to Gyp and held the door open for Petra and there was a new understanding between them as they walked out into the yard.

"You can see now that it would have taken you quite a long time to get here by yourself the other night," he remarked. "If we climb up here you can look out across the two valleys."

The path was steep and he held out his hand again to grip her own and again the sensation of quivering excitement ran through her. This man was dangerously attractive. She tried to fix her mind on the friendship that seemed newly to have sprung up between them but there were other feelings surging inside her.

"Look – the sun is setting," Gareth said.

They had reached a high plateau of short, sweet grass from which she looked down at the roof of *Ty Coch* and the narrow road that ran like a tightly-stretched ribbon over the cliff-top. The lake below shone darkly and the clouds above were scarlet-tipped.

"I used to come up here with Eleri," Gareth said. "We

would climb up here and sit, just sit and say nothing at all. When I was expecting her, I'd come here and wait. If she'd been over at *Ty Mawr*, she would come along the cliff road. Other times she would walk across the meadow. I'd see her like a dot, at first, and then no bigger than my finger, running across the landscape. And when she got nearer, she would look up and wave her hand. I knew she was smiling, then. Oh, she had a smile to draw the heart out of a man.''

"Eleri is dead," Petra said, her voice flat with emotion. "You should let her rest, leave her in peace."

"But she won't let *me* find peace!" He swung about to face her, his hands gripping her shoulders.

"She died, you see. She died of her own will, without any explanation. That tears at me! Not to know. Never to know *why*!''

"You should try to put it out of your head," Petra pleaded.

"I did. Oh, I did! For years she was no more than a shadow in my mind, and then you came. You came out of the mist at the edge of the dark water and you looked like her. Did you know that you looked like her, Petra Cunningham? Did you know that?"

She made no reply, for his mouth fastened on hers and she was no longer her own keeper. She was melting into the closeness of him, feeling his need for her, and she closed her eyes, her arms stealing about his neck.

"Oh, Petra. Petra, *cariad* ..."

Then abruptly he pushed her away, and his voice rose into the wind that whipped about them.

"Why did you have to come? Why do you have to look like her and yet not like her? Why do you make me feel as I've not felt for years when I've no right – ''

"Gareth – please?" She stared at him in bewilderment,

his sudden rejection of her like a cruel blow. "I – I don't understand ..."

"Eleri was engaged to me," he ground. "She was going to marry me and she died. I've tried hard all these years not to admit it, but likely she died of her own choosing. She threw herself in the lake, rather than marry me, and there's nothing so certain, no matter how I try to deny it." He shrugged his shoulders and his hands dropped to his sides in a gesture of surrender. "Do you understand that I haven't the right to offer anything to any other woman," he whispered, "until I know the truth of it?"

"But I'm not Eleri and I'm not any other woman," Petra cried, her whole body throbbing with the hurt of his refusal. "I'm *me*, Gareth, and I don't even look much like her. You think I do because when you look at me you are really looking at *her*, at the girl who died! You see her as she is in your memory – always nineteen. But she's been dead *ten years*, and if she really did kill herself, what right do you have to take all the guilt upon yourself?"

"I don't. If I ever found the reason I'd be free, gladly free!"

"I see." Petra closed her eyes despairingly, her voice low, defeated. "So until the truth comes out you'll still be bound to a memory, as much bound to her as if you'd both died together that night. And it may be years, Gareth, if at all, before you find the truth of it. Am I to wait until then?"

"Wait? I never asked you to wait ..." His voice was harsh and dangerously low.

She stared at him as though he had struck her, indignation flushing into embarrassment. Of course he hadn't asked her, but he had held her with tenderness, kissed her with such passion that she had allowed herself to believe that he, too, felt the same stirrings of love and longing. But he had thought of Eleri as he kissed her and the unmistakable need of his body had been aroused by the memory of a lost love.

Petra tore herself from his side and started down the path, running heedlessly. Behind her he shouted,

"Petra! Petra, *cariad*! Wait! I'll help you down!"

The sky had suddenly darkened, and through her angry tears the lake below was sinister and still.

"No!" she cried, without turning her head. "No. I don't want you!"

By some small miracle she reached level ground unharmed and ran towards her car. Tears of humiliation ran down her cheeks and her lips were quivering. She had betrayed feelings that she had not even realised she possessed. She had surrendered to them, offered them gladly to Gareth Davies, and he had thrown them back in her face.

Her hands shook as she fitted the key into the ignition of the car. She wiped her eyes on the sleeve of her sweater and backed out of the yard, avoiding a furiously barking Gyp.

Gareth had stayed where he was. As she drove under the lee of the hill, she glanced up and saw him, standing tall with the wind in his hair and his head turned in the direction of the dark water.

Petra drove faster, accelerating onto the upper road, fighting back her sobs. It was useless to try to get near a man like Gareth Davies. You couldn't love his sort. Why, she wasn't even sure now that she wanted to. She would forget him, that's what she would do! Push him out of her mind and accept that they would never get on.

Him and me, she thought, we're fire and ice. We are of opposing elements that don't mix. But which of us is of fire, she pondered sadly as she drew in a deep, calming breath, and which one is ice?

There was a car parked outside *Ty Mawr*, and Petra stared at its sleek, shining lines in dismay, sure for a moment that Edward Bonner had returned. Desperately she dabbed at her eyes and with shaking hand outlined her lips afresh with colour.

She saw his shadow, long and dark, before she saw him, then a figure emerged from the screening bushes at the side of the house.

"Hi there, darling!" The voice was familiar, its lazy drawl unmistakable.

"Simon!" She was out of the car in a flash. "I didn't recognise your car for a moment. How long have you been waiting? Why didn't you write? Why didn't you let me know you were coming?"

"Oh, you know me, and anyway, it was quicker to drive up here. I wanted to surprise you. Did I?"

He kissed her lightly and if he noticed her wet cheeks he made no comment. Holding her at arms' length he said,

"My, my, but we have gone countrified, haven't we? What have you been doing to your hair?"

"Nothing ..."

"Hmm. Exactly. And is this the ancestral shack?" He laid his arm lightly around her shoulders and looked afresh at the house.

"That's right. And most of the valley, of course, and eight cottages ..."

He nodded, seemingly with approval, but his face was inscrutable and his eyes told her nothing.

"Am I to be asked in? I could use a large, cold drink. It's been a long, boring haul from London and the roads round here are like corkscrews."

"Yes. Of course. Er – do come in."

They sounded like polite strangers. She flushed and fumbled in her bag for the door-key. It irritated her to

discover that her fingers still trembled, but she tilted her
chin and walked up the steps ahead of him. Over her
shoulder she said brightly,

"Oh, Simon, it really is wonderful to see you!"

And hoped that she believed it and that Simon believed
it, too.

Petra had eaten little of the meal she cooked for them and
now she and Simon were in the sitting-room, he lounging
with a glass of whisky at his elbow, she in a chair opposite.
With the curtains drawn and the lamplight glowing, the
scene was one of cosy domesticity.

"So this is the heart of your great-uncle's kingdom?"

"You'll have to see all the house when it's light," Petra
said eagerly, ignoring the faint amusement in his voice.

"My love, I had a quick look around while I was waiting
for you. The place is more like an antiquated barn than
anything else."

"Simon! It's a lovely old house," she protested. "Uncle
Ifor was very happy here, I know it. He used to own the
quarry, you know, but it's run down now and most of the
people round these parts are farmers."

"Oh, is that what they do? I did see some scrubby
looking sheep ..."

"Did you drive through the village, Simon?" She was
determined not to rise to his mocking bait.

"Yes, I did, and very nearly missed it. One street, a
chapel, a garage, a shop, and a pub about a mile down the
road. Hardly Las Vegas."

"It's not supposed to be," she jerked, hurt and
bewildered by his attitude.

"Sweetheart, I'm not criticising the place. I'm sure it's a
charming part of the world if you're very old and tired of

life," he smiled.

"Like Edward Bonner's friends?" she mused, half to herself.

"Like who's friends?" He glanced up with sudden alertness.

"Edward Bonner's. Bonner offered to buy *Ty Mawr* on behalf of some friends of his who are retiring."

"They didn't approach you directly?"

"No. Bonner says the husband was something in public life and wants to remain incognito."

"That's sometimes done." Simon drained his glass and held it out to be refilled. "Of course, it's none of my business, but was it a decent offer?"

"Fifty thousand pounds."

"You're kidding!"

"No, I'm not. And after I turned it down – "

"You *turned down* fifty thousand pounds?"

"Yes," she nodded, "and he came back and offered sixty thousand."

"There's a clever girl!" His pleasure was evident. "But you can't hold out for much more. Likely he'll not go higher."

"I wasn't holding out for more, Simon. I turned down the sixty thousand, too."

"But you must be out of your tiny mind!" he exclaimed, his face registering disbelief. "You'll never get a better offer in a million years! It's the back of beyond, Petra. The place is dead!"

"I don't care!" she flung indignantly. "I like it here. It's peaceful and unspoiled, and that's the way it's going to stay! And the house is comfortable and warm and it's got enough mod. cons. to satisfy even *you*, Simon!"

"Except a phone."

"Uncle Ifor disliked telephones."

"Or a garage."

"He didn't need one. He didn't drive. And anyway, there's plenty of outbuildings and a barn." She puckered her forehead into a frown and said, "I suppose the property would be worth far more in the South."

"Maybe so, but the whole point is that this isn't in the South. It's in a God-forsaken corner of a little bit of mountain where the people don't even bother to learn English properly! You'll never sell it for more than sixty thousand, believe me. The land isn't up to much, if you ask me, and that valley looks as if it could flood at the drop of a hat, as well."

"Thanks for the vote of confidence," she hissed, then closing her eyes and mentally counting to ten she said, more calmly, "There are the cottages. I told you, didn't I that there's a regular income from them?"

"That's something, I suppose ..."

"It's forty pounds a week!" Petra supplied, preparing to defend *Ty Mawr* to the Last Call. "Of course, Bill Jones Post Office takes ten percent and I've got rates to pay and repairs to do, but it's not bad."

"It's daylight robbery. Nobody in their senses asks five pounds a week for the rental of a cottage! And what was all that about grazing rights?"

"Well – er – some of the farmers graze their cattle on *Ty Mawr* land," she defended, wilting a little under the merciless probing. "The pasture is good, there, better than most other places. Uncle Ifor always allowed free grazing and I can see no reason why I.shouldn't do the same," she ended, lamely.

"And that made your Uncle Ifor a very popular old man, I shouldn't wonder."

"He was," she said, stiffly. "And the people here welcomed me here for his sake when I first came. But now I think they're beginning to accept me for my own."

"You talk as if you want them to like you. You sound like Mr Bonner's friends – about to retire from the world." His voice held a teasing quality, now, and it seemed to Petra that Simon was trying new tactics.

"Not retire," she protested. "Oh, Simon, this is the most beautiful place. When you've been here for a few days, the peace will get to you, too."

"Doubtless it would, my love, if I were to stay that long; but I have to be back in London by tomorrow evening."

"So soon? But I thought you would stay for a couple of days, at least."

"Sorry, sweetie. There's an advertising drive on for the new perfume I told you about. I've roughed out a few sketches – "

"You got the contract? Oh, Simon, I'm so glad."

"Thanks." He nodded with mock modesty. "Their Sales Director seems to like my initial ideas. I'm having a meal with him tomorrow night, so I must get back, you see. Why don't you come along with me?"

"But I'm not due back yet and besides, I'm not at all sure that I'm ever going back."

"You're not serious? You can't rusticate here. Petra, sweet, you can't possibly!"

"I can, Simon. I feel at home here. My roots are here, I know it. My grandmother was born in this house, you know."

"And ran away pretty damn' quick and never came back!"

Petra tossed her head. "Well, I'm more like Uncle Ifor than my grandmother," she countered obstinately. "She ran away and I have come back. I belong at *Ty Mawr*. I want to live here," she finished breathlessly, "always."

"I see." He watched her from beneath his thick, fair lashes. "I don't want to spoil your dream, my love, but is there any place for me in all this?"

"Yes, of course. Of course there is." She spoke quickly. "You're very artistic, Simon. I've always said it. You're wasted in commercial advertising. You could paint, here. The mountains are so beautiful, so very beautiful."

"Look – are you seriously telling me that I'm supposed to rusticate here with you, painting scenic views for the tourists?" he demanded, hotly.

"You have to do what you want to do," Petra pleaded. "We each of us have to be free."

Soon, she thought, we will be quarrelling.

"Hey, Miss Cunningham! Do I detect a whiff of Women's Lib.? Petra, love, what's got into you these last few days?"

"Please, Simon, I'm serious. I want to live here at *Ty Mawr*, to become part of the community. I want it more than anything. But we could compromise. We could spend part of the year here if you'd like, and the rest of the time in London. I'm trying to be reasonable, darling ..."

"Then you're not succeeding very well," he retorted, "and you're not being very practical, either. This great place would be far too big for just the two of us – "

Just the two of us, she echoed mutely. No children, then? No babies between us, Simon?

"Uncle Ifor lived here alone and he got along all right!"

She jumped to her feet, tossing her head, flouncing like a child to the long window that overlooked the side of the house and the riverbank. A purple twilight gentled the trees and blotted out the mountain tops. A night bird cried and in the distance, a dog barked. As far as she could see, there were no lights visible – just trees silhouetted against the deepening sky and the blur of the ragged hedge that once had marked the boundary of the kitchen garden.

We are quarrelling, she thought dismally. She pushed shut the window and pulled over the curtains.

"Oh Simon, I'm sorry," she whispered, walking back to the fireside, reaching for his glass. "But you've often said how sick you are of the rat-race ..."

"I know. I know, my love. But sixty thousand pounds isn't to be sniffed at, you know. Why, with that kind of money, you could afford a nice little place – in Wales, if you must – that we could use for weekends and holidays. Surely that's more sensible?"

But she didn't want to be sensible, Petra thought childishly. She wanted Simon to feel as she did, the spell of the high peaks and the winding river. She wanted him to love it as Gareth loved it.

"It's late," she said, dully, "and I'm tired. I'll show you where you're sleeping."

He rose easily to his feet, a small smile moving his lips.

"Still observing the conventions? Still playing hard to get, Petra? Why do you do it?"

He reached out for her, pulling her to him, kissing her lightly on brow and cheeks. His hands were cool and he smelled of aftershave. His lips were undemanding. Petra closed her eyes and willed herself to feel pleasure.

"I'm getting nowhere – fast!" he mocked lightly. "Show me to my solitary bed, then."

"You're in Uncle Ifor's room. You'll like it."

"So long as the old boy doesn't haunt it?"

"Of course he doesn't!" She spoke rapidly. "It's a lovely room. If you hear any noises, it'll be the cat!"

She showed him the room, held up her face for his goodnight kiss then walked quickly back across the gallery to her own bedroom, wishing she didn't feel as if she had been granted a reprieve from something she couldn't quite put her finger on. Simon was as handsome and attractive as ever, but his slightly contemptuous amusement grated on her. He was, she thought, too smoothly charming for this rugged countryside.

She walked over to the window and stood for a while, looking out into the night. She wondered if Gareth was in bed and if he was sleeping soundly. Or was his sleep tormented by dreams of the dark water? Did Eleri's pale little wraith keep watch beside *Ty Coch*, and did he turn and cry out to her? Petra shook herself mentally. After what had happened on the plateau between them, it was most certainly none of her concern she reminded herself irritably.

She was too restless to sleep properly. The house seemed too big and too quiet. It seemed to brood, as if Simon's criticism had seeped into its very stones and hurt it. Strange that when she was alone in it, Petra mused, its size never bothered her. After pummelling her pillow yet again, she got up, slipped on her housecoat and padded on bare feet along the corridor.

"Looking for me, sweetheart?"

Simon, in dressing gown and slippers, came out of the bathroom at the other end of the corridor.

"I'm going downstairs to get a book," she said, wishing her voice didn't sound so stiff and unfriendly.

"You'd find me far more entertaining than a book, Petra."

"Good-*night*, Simon! See you in the morning."

He shrugged, tossed her his mocking smile and went into the master-bedroom.

She was halfway down the stairs when the song began, echoing round the hall in the high, sweet voice of a child.

'One, two, three, Eleri,
I saw Mother Carey,
Waving wand for imp and fairy,
Down in the valley ...'

Eight

"No! Oh, no!"

Petra crouched against the wall, hands over her ears, but nothing could shut out the singing or the trills of rippling laughter that followed it.

Simultaneously Simon's voice rose in angry alarm as his door crashed open.

"What the devil was that?"

"Eleri," Petra whispered through shaking lips. "It was Eleri."

"Who? Where is she?"

"She's not here. She's dead – long ago," she gasped, fighting against a sudden hysterical desire to laugh out loud. "Eleri's been dead for ten years!"

"Now look here, Petra – what's the game?" He glared down at her from the top of the stairs. "If this is some stupid trick – "

"No trick," she jerked, pulling herself to her feet and walking shakily towards him. "Megan Pritchard – the woman who works here – had a niece called Eleri. Eleri used to come over to *Ty Mawr* a lot to keep my uncle company. He was very fond of her."

"In one of the bedrooms – all those things – are they hers?"

"Yes."

"But you said she was dead?"

"She is. Ten years ago, on the night before her wedding. She was drowned in the lake over in the next valley. They brought in a verdict of 'Misadventure', but there's a chance she meant to do it. She was only nineteen." Petra drew a deep breath and continued shakily. "The first night I was here I heard the singing. I was sleeping in the room you've got and I told myself afterwards it had been a nightmare. But you heard it too, didn't you?"

"Too loudly for comfort," Simon admitted wryly.

"Then do you think that it's just remotely possible that if someone has been happy in a place, some echo of them might remain there and be triggered off at certain times?" she asked, doubtfully.

"Half an hour ago I'd have said not," he answered, "but now I just don't know. I really don't know what to think." Then he shrugged and smiled wanly. "Anyway, it's gone now, whatever it was, so away back to bed with you, there's a good girl."

"Oh Simon, no!" Her eyes widened with renewed apprehension. "I'm afraid. I shan't sleep, I know I shan't!"

"Then take a sleeping pill."

"I don't have any," she whispered ruefully.

"Hang on. I'll give you a couple." He patted her shoulder and went back into the lamplit bedroom, emerging a few moments later with two white tablets in the palm of his hand.

"Swallow these down," he urged, "and I guarantee you'll not hear even a choir of ghosts, unless of course, you'd care to ...?"

He left the invitation unfinished and regarded her with one eyebrow raised suggestively, but Petra shook her head, held out her hand for the tablets and went back to her room. This was neither the time nor the place she thought defensively and anyway, she didn't want to. It was as simple as that.

"Swallow them down, then," Simon said, appearing in the doorway. "I'll stay with you, if you like, until you're asleep."

She smiled at him gratefully and did as he told her.

"You're very sweet," she smiled, pulling the blankets up to her chin.

"I'm a fool," he grunted, settling himself on the window-seat. "Close your eyes. You'll be all right, now, and we'll have a talk about all this in the morning."

Whatever the pills were, Petra thought drowsily, they certainly seemed to work well. Within a very short time her eyelids began to droop, her limbs to grow heavy. A few minutes more and she was deeply asleep.

Morning came too abruptly, or so it seemed when the light struck Petra's closed eyes and she struggled up into wakefulness. Simon was standing beside her bed, a tray of tea in his hands.

"Oh, I meant to get up and cook you some breakfast," she protested sleepily.

"No need, my love. You know I never eat it. Sit up and drink this."

He handed her a cup of tea then settled himself at the end of the bed and gazed at her quizzically.

"Did you sleep well?" she ventured.

"No, not very," he admitted. "To be honest, this place has begun to give me the creeps. If anyone had asked me, I'd say the supernatural was a load of old rubbish, but between you and me, darling, I'll be glad when we're both out of here. Who told you about this Eleri?''

"Gar – Mr Davies.''

"Who's he, then?''

"The farmer who lives in the next valley. He was the one Eleri was going to marry.''

"And he confided the sad story to you?''

"He talked about it," she said, reluctantly.

"You've certainly got your feet under the table, Petra. Does he turn·you on, this *Mr* Davies?''

"He's rather a surly character. Moody, too," she evaded.

"Look darling, I've no legal claim on you yet," he said, lightly, "but I don't much like the idea of you running over to swap confidences with a love-lorn sheep-farmer. You'd better get up now, or you'll have no time to pack.''

"Pack?'' she stared at him, bewildered.

"Pack,'' he confirmed. "You're not staying on here any longer after last night's carry-on. Whoever that thing was, it wasn't something I'd care to have you hear again when you're all by yourself in this great place.''

"I'm not afraid.''

"Nonsense! You were terrified last night and don't try to deny it. You were shaking from head to foot.''

"That was last night.''

"And if you hear it again tonight? My dear girl, it'll start all over again. And you'd be alone and I couldn't bear that.''

"Darling, it's very sweet of you, but I'm staying," Petra whispered. "It did give me a fright at first, but I'll get over it. I'll *have* to get over it. Oh, there's no need for you to worry." She reached for his hand and squeezed it affectionately. "And now, if you don't mind, I want to get up. I'd like to show you some of the countryside, and we can call in and see Megan.''

"My love, there simply isn't time," he said, regretfully. "I must be off well before lunch. I can't risk being late and losing the chance of that contract. Make yourself glamorous!" He mouthed her a kiss, and went out.

Petra still felt heavy-eyed and a little stupid, as if the pills she had swallowed the night before had slowed down her brain, but when she had taken a shower and cleaned her teeth, she began to feel better. Simon hadn't liked her countrified appearance so, with some idea of gaining his approval, she put on a slender dress of green wool, belted with Mexican leather, and drew her hair to the back of her head with a matching comb.

"You look very lovely," were his first words when she walked into the kitchen.

Simon always noticed what women wore and was quick to compliment her on anything new or a different hair-style, Petra thought appreciatively. He remembered birthdays, too, and booked the best seats at theatres and restaurants.

"Does the dress mean you've changed your mind?" he asked, one eyebrow raised.

"Darling – sorry, but I can't come back with you." Her face showed plainly her distress. "I want to stay here. I can't explain it, but I have a feeling I was meant to stay. Uncle Ifor left this place to me because he wanted me to love it as much as he loved it. And I do, in spite of everything. Don't you see? I just *mustn't* be afraid?"

"No, I don't see, but one thing I'm certain of, Petra. Something – or *someone* – has certainly captured your imagination," he retorted, tersely. "Could it be the sheep-farmer? Could it be that Davies fellow you were talking about? I knew from the way you spoke about him that he was something more than a neighbour."

"That's ridiculous!" Wide-eyed, she flung round to face him.

"You think so? A man doesn't start talking about his last love until a new one comes over the horizon. And you're a pushover for a sob-story, Petra. Admit it! You'll dig into your pocket for any old charity that comes along and you're the only one who'd feed a cat that came and squatted here." He nodded with distaste at Moggy, who had just stalked in, his tail held high.

"You're imagining things! I don't even like Gareth Davies," Petra flung, trying hard to keep her voice even. "He's very rude and insolent, not in the least friendly like the rest of the villagers. He looks upon me as a foreigner."

"I see. And I suppose that's why he told you all about his sad love-affair?"

"He mentioned it, that's all."

"And you've felt sorry for him ever since," Simon reasoned. "Just as you've felt sorry for your old uncle and built him up in your mind into a romantic picture of a dear old gentleman, whereas the truth is that he was probably a sour old eccentric. After all, he knew where you lived; he could have got in touch with you years ago, but he never bothered. And now he's saddled you with a haunted house, land on which everyone else grazes his livestock and eight cottages let at damn nearly a peppercorn rent. It's time you woke up to reality, Petra, and grabbed that sixty thousand pounds!"

"Don't lecture me, Simon," she said, wearily.

"Sweetheart, I'm sorry." He sounded genuinely contrite. "I shouldn't be angry with you. I wanted us to enjoy this weekend. But I do worry about you, you know. I worry about you very much, my darling, because I do happen to be in love with you."

He placed his hands on her waist and drew her to him.

"Yes. Yes, I know."

She wanted to say that she loved him too, but the words

wouldn't come. Instead she raised her face obediently for his kiss, closing her eyes, wishing yet again that she could feel something deeper than pleasure.

"Change your mind?" Simon was whispering. "Change your mind and come to London with me today? Forget this place? Give it up, Petra. You'll have to, in the end ..."

"No, Simon. It's no use. If I came back with you now I'd always wonder if I had done the right thing. You must give me time to make up my own mind."

"All right. Have it your own way." He stepped back and regarded her gravely. "I won't rush you into anything, but I promise you though, that I'll not give up trying to persuade you."

She smiled up at him, grateful for his understanding.

"I'll drive down to Betws-y-Coed with you," she offered. "At least you can see the Swallow Falls before you go and we could have some coffee, there. Or would you rather stop off in the village and meet Megan? She's hurt her ankle but she'll be back with me on Monday."

"I'm delighted for the dear lady, but don't inflict her on me," he begged.

"Very well." She hid her disappointment and went to get the green coat that matched her dress.

"Don't you think the house looks lovely in the sunlight?" she couldn't resist asking as he carried his bag out to his car.

"Very pretty, sweet. Very picturesque. Now please take the worshipping look off your face and look at me instead. I want to kiss you again. I don't suppose we'll get another chance to be alone until you get back to town. And you *are* coming back, you know. You've got a kind of spring-fever and you need to get it out of your system."

She would have protested again, but he was holding her

tightly, kissing her lingeringly. When he finally released her, his expression was thoughtful.

"Remember that I want to marry you," he said, lightly, "and that I've got my work to consider as well as your whims and fancies. Are you going to show me the way?"

"Yes, of course." She slammed shut his door, then somewhat chastened, got into her own car.

She was a little ashamed of the relief that gripped her when, having enjoyed an excellent cup of coffee at a wayside cafe, they came out again into the sunshine.

Simon had been a charming companion, not once mentioning the offer she had received for *Ty Mawr*. He had talked instead of the new contract he hoped to land, agreed that the Swallow Falls with the trees bursting into leaf all around and the water cascading over the brown rocks were well worth a visit and promised dutifully to look in on her two flatmates to persuade them to write.

"But I'm hoping you'll be back in your own world long before they get round to putting pen to paper," he said. "Take care of yourself, my love. I do worry about you all alone, you know."

"I know you do, and I'm grateful," she said contritely, wishing at the same time that he hadn't reminded her of the singing and the laughing and the night ahead.

"Grateful?" He lifted his brows then flicked her cheek with an elegant finger. "I am hoping for more than gratitude from you. I didn't exactly enjoy last night, you know. It wasn't easy to sleep, knowing you were so near, so afraid. 'Bye, Petra."

He gave her another light kiss and got into his car. As she waved, the relief that filled her was mingled with guilt. Simon loved her and she ought to have had better sense than to spring her wishes on him without warning. Perhaps they both needed time to think!

She returned slowly to *Ty Mawr*. It was strange, but the winding road was already as familiar as if she had been travelling along it all her life. The sun was almost at its height and the landscape was blossoming into a loveliness that caught at her heart. The mountains no longer threatened, but beckoned her gently and the slopes beneath, with their outcroppings of blue-veined slate, were fast becoming a source of strength.

That night, as if to deny the promise of the morning, the mist came down again. Petra had spent the afternoon in the garden, clearing weeds from some clumps of shyly emerging primroses. She had never had the chance to grub about in a garden before, and by the time the light began to fail, she was surprised to find how tired and hungry she was.

She washed her earth-caked hands, then cooked herself an omelette, opened a tin of fruit and carried it on a tray through to the sitting-room. There was a film on television and she settled down contentedly to watch it. It was, she supposed, a good film, but the images seemed even more unreal than usual, while the plot was so hard to follow that after a while she gave up trying, and let the scenes succeed one another without listening closely to any one of them.

Moggy pattered in, ignored her greeting and curled up in a corner of the settee. The mist was rising, or perhaps descending would have been a better word, Petra thought wryly, for it did look as if a blanket was being thrown down from the mountain tops.

Petra snapped off the television and crossed over to the window to draw the curtains. The neglected garden, the crumbling walls, the uneven track leading through the high gateposts to the water meadows beyond, were shrouded in grey mist that billowed about the house.

Something or someone moved on the fringe of the rolling cloud. She caught her breath sharply and moved closer to the window, eyes narrowed. Whatever it was out there was anxious not to be seen, for an instant later the mist rolled down again and the figure was gone.

"Moggy, I think my imagination is playing tricks on me," she said.

Moggy yawned, showing a pink tongue.

"There is something very reassuring about a cat," Petra continued, piling up the dishes and preparing to carry them back to the kitchen. "Cats don't expect to be led about like dogs. They're independent souls who stay only where they feel comfortable and if Moggy is comfortable here, there is no reason at all why *I* shouldn't be."

Her own voice echoed faintly back to her as she crossed the slate-floored hall. Simon would be amused and astonished to hear her talking to herself. He would probably predict darkly that in a few years she would be as eccentric as Old Ifor.

The dishes washed and dried, she checked the locks on front and back doors and walked slowly upstairs, the friendliness of the house enfolding her. She looked in at the open door of the master bedroom. Simon had folded the sheets and blankets neatly, and the room had the air of any apartment vacated by an overnight guest.

Her own room was less neat. She made the bed and turned down the radiator. It was still early. In London, she seldom went to bed before midnight, but in London she never ached with a healthy tiredness that was immensely satisfying.

The room tidy, she went over to close the window. Through the small gap, fingers of mist were creeping. In the garden below, something moved again, but it might have been mist shifting slowly about a tree and giving it the semblance of life.

Then suddenly, somewhere in the still corridor beyond, a child began to cry. Unbelieving, Petra whipped round, her eyes upon the half-open door, her mouth dry with shock.

"Oh, no! No!" she whispered with lips tight with terror. "Please, not again?"

The crying was heart-rending, unearthly. Somewhere a child was sobbing as if its heart was broken. It was the thought of that heartbreak which drew Petra into the corridor. No child, unearthly or not, should have cause to weep like that.

The sound came from everywhere and nowhere. It was in the air about her, beating on her eardrums. She heard her own voice, shrill with panic, crying,

"Where are you? What do you want? *What do you want?*"

Abruptly as it had begun, the crying ceased, only to be replaced by a high-pitched, demented giggling that went on and on and on.

Head down, hands on ears, Petra ran blindly along the gallery and down the stairs. Her heels tapped an uneven rhythm across the floor and her hands were wet with sweat as she tugged open the heavy front door. The dim shape of her car loomed through the mist. She ran to it and bent to the handle of the door. It was locked. The keys were in her handbag and her handbag was in her bedroom. To get those keys, she must brave the stairs and the giggling, crying creature in the upper corridor. As she stared at the house, its door wide open, the light in her bedroom went out.

Speechless, she turned and fled into the mist, stumbling along the uneven track. Something barred her way. She tried to scream and could not; she tried to swerve, tripped, and was held fast.

"Taking another short cut?" Gareth Davies asked.

His voice was mocking, but he was warm and human and solid and she clung to his strength, weakly sobbing.

"*Diawl!* But you are in a state, aren't you?" he said. "What happened? You're shaking – "

"In the house!" She tried to control her chattering teeth. "Something – someone – Eleri is there. She's crying and laughing. I heard it!"

"Have you been drinking?"

"No! No! I tell you *I heard it!* I was running – "

"Straight into the river, by the looks of things. Come on, now. We'll go and have a look around."

His voice had changed, and now he spoke to her as if he were coaxing a timid child, indulging it, pretending to believe.

"I'm not going back there," she hissed, but he interrupted her with an impatient little shake.

"And you can't stay out here all night, now can you? I'll find out what's wrong for you."

"The light in my room went out," she sobbed.

"I'll take care of that, too." Again the coaxing words. "Come on, now, there's a good girl."

She submitted to being led back into the hall. She was past caring any longer.

Gareth tilted his head. "I can't hear anything."

"Well, *I* heard it! First the crying like a lost child and then the giggling. It was awful and I *did* hear it!"

"What say we have a good stiff drink first," he said with decision, piloting her into the sitting-room.

"I don't drink whisky," she protested as he pushed her gently into a chair and busied himself with the decanter.

"Tonight you do," he said firmly. "Toss it back now, and don't argue."

The liquid scorched her throat but her shaking lessened.

Gareth bent and re-filled her glass.

"Stay there and I'll go up and see what's to be seen," he said, patting her shoulder as he went out. Like I was a dog, she thought wildly, wanting to laugh hysterically. But she didn't laugh. She couldn't. She was past laughing, past caring, past worrying. She gulped again at her drink. She didn't like it but it had a calming effect.

"Everywhere's quiet," Gareth said, appearing a few minutes later. "There's nobody else in the house."

"The light in my bedroom?"

He held up a light bulb, shaking it so that it tinkled.

"Burned out," he said, smiling. "Sheer coincidence. I've taken one from another bedroom for now. It's all right. Nothing to worry about any more."

"But there *is*. There *was* something. I heard it, and last night Simon heard the singing."

"Simon? Your boyfriend's been, then?" He threw her a surprised look.

"He was here last night, waiting, when I – when I got back from your place." Remembering Gareth's kiss, she stammered a little. "He had to get back to London today. I'm surprised Myfi Chester didn't tell you. I went with him as far as Betws-y-Coed."

"I've not been to the village today. There was a sale over at Llanberis. I went to that."

"Simon heard the singing," Petra insisted. "He was worried about leaving me alone here."

"A voice can't harm you."

"*You* didn't hear it," she accused.

"Are you going to be all right now, or do you want me to stay?" he asked.

With all her heart she wanted to say yes. She wanted to stay close to his strength, his manliness. She wanted, during the long, dark night, to be able to reach out for him and find him beside her, but remnants of foolish pride still clung to her.

"I'll be fine," she assured him, lightly. "But the mist is very thick. How will you get back?"

"I walked over. I'll walk back."

"Then it must have been you I saw earlier. Was it you? Why didn't you come in?"

"I wasn't sure of my welcome," he admitted frankly. "The manner of our parting yesterday was – well, I'm sorry for it, because you offered me friendship and I had nothing to give you in return. Nothing but doubts and suspicions, that is ..."

"Suspicions?"

"You had been talking to Edward Bonner. I was pretty sure you'd accept his offer."

"Well I didn't. I'm not selling. I thought I'd told you. I'm staying at *Ty Mawr*."

"In spite of everything? Then you do belong." He gave her a long look then said,

"The room where Eleri's things were stored is open now."

"Megan gave me the key."

"Then that explains something else. Mother Carey came over to my place last night, babbling about seeing Eleri in her wedding veil at the window."

"So you came over to see if it was true? You didn't come to see me, then?"

"My motives were mixed, but I think I can guess now."

"I tried on the veil," Petra said. "I'm sorry if it was in bad taste, but I did it on an impulse."

"Eleri often stayed here. Old Ifor kept her room as a sort of shrine," Gareth said. "I don't think he went into it very often himself, after she died, but Megan kept it clean. The old man was very fond of the Pritchards. They were almost family to him. He was pleased when Eleri and I decided to get married."

"Does the symbol of an eye, a red-pupilled eye, mean anything to you?" Petra asked abruptly, seeking desperately to change the drift of their conversation, trying by any means to keep his safeness with her.

"Round here, you mean?" He frowned for a moment then smiled. "You're thinking about the cursing well down in the old quarry."

"What on earth is a cursing well?"

"Oh, they were quite commonplace round these parts at one time, right up to the turn of the century. People who wanted anybody cursed threw the name of their enemy into a pool and paid a fee to the one who guarded the pool. There's one like that at the quarry. It's dried up, now, has been ever since I can remember, but it has an eye painted on the rock above it."

"It sounds creepy."

"Oh, I don't think so. That particular spot has become the local courting place. Boys and girls go there to – well, to be boys and girls. I never went there myself. It's a gloomy place and there's a danger of rock falls."

So he had never taken Eleri there, Petra mused, which could only mean that she had gone there with someone else. And whatever had happened there had led to the painting of that strange, haunting picture.

"Why do you want to know about the cursing well?" he asked.

"Oh, it was something that someone said," Petra said, deliberately vague.

"Some of these old superstitions die hard," Gareth shrugged. "Are you sure you'll be all right if I go back now?"

"Yes, of course." The moment of intimacy over she rose to her feet, holding out her hand politely. It was useless to try to keep him, she thought sadly, useless and foolish. "You've been very kind and I'm sorry I acted so stupidly. But I *did* hear the voice, Gareth."

"Then if you hear it again, come over to *Ty Coch*," he returned, "and if the mist is too thick, then lock your bedroom door and stick it out till morning."

It was clear that he still only half believed her story. In any event, he would have been too far away from the house to have heard anything, even when she had opened the door, Petra realised.

"You really are staying on at *Ty Mawr*, then? The village doesn't have to worry?"

"I'm staying," she said, wondering why the matter should cause anyone any worry. But he merely smiled, then turned abruptly and strode back into the hall. The front door closed behind him and Petra stood very still, her heart thudding with apprehension again, dreading to hear the weeping and the giggling once more. But everywhere was peaceful, as if nothing had ever happened.

Moggy was still sleeping by the sitting-room fire and Petra threw on more logs and placed the guard in position. Then slipping off her shoes she curled up on the sofa. Not for anything would she climb those echoing stairs again until daybreak.

Nine

Petra awoke to the realisation that it was Sunday. The sunshine of the previous day had gone but there were glimpses of blue sky between the clouds.

She stretched each limb painstakingly. She had slept well, for the room had been warm, the long settee comfortable. Only once had she awakened in the night, to hear Moggy's rhythmic purring close to her ear. The gentle sound comforted her and she had immediately fallen back into a deep sleep.

Now, something within her made her decide that she would go to chapel. If she really intended to stay in the valley, then she must begin to take her place in the life of the village. She tried not to think of Simon's ridicule if he had known of her intention, for Simon had no strong beliefs, save in himself. Now, as she wandered round the room, drawing back the curtains, switching off the lamp she had left burning all night, she wondered if that philosophy would satisfy her, or if coming to the valley had aroused in her the need to worship something bigger than herself, something strong and powerful that was the source of what lay beneath the mountains, above the peaks.

And there was another reason for her need. She wanted to ask for help. She loved *Ty Mawr* and longed to live there always. In the daylight, when the sunlight played on the river and the blackbird sang in the cherry tree, she could make light of her fancies, invent a dozen good reasons why the singing and the laughing were only part of a waking dream. But at nightfall, when the shadows lengthened and the birdsong was hushed and the silence about her so complete that it throbbed inside her head, then she knew she was not dreaming. Then she knew the voices were not of her imagining, and she was afraid. Perhaps, in chapel, she could find a reason, sort it all out. She hoped she would. More than anything, almost, she hoped she could.

She bathed then dressed carefully, choosing the cream-coloured outfit she had worn on her arrival and adding a small green beret, for she was fairly certain that the women of the valley would always wear hats to chapel.

The service would probably begin at about ten, she reasoned, but if she was too early, then she could call in and see Megan. The idea pleased her and she hummed a remembered snatch of hymn from her childhood as she made coffee and toast in the kitchen.

When she closed the front door behind her, Petra stood for a while on the topmost step, drinking in the morning. The mist had almost cleared, but the air was damp and cool and the young leaves hung limply in the windless air.

She drove slowly down the broad track, between the high gateposts and into the meadow. The river was high, running swiftly between its willow-thick banks. To her left, the grass sloped gently to the foot of the mountain, its peak hidden in thick white cloud. But lower down, the lingering mist writhed and twisted into fantastic and beautiful shapes and she felt again the peace of it all and the longing to be a part of it.

At the top of the street, Petra parked her car. Several

villagers were hurrying across the square into the chapel and she joined them, nodding a smiling good-morning as she recognised one or two of the people she had met at the *Noson Lawen*. But strangely nobody returned her greeting and, with an uncomfortable feeling of having been put in her place, Petra walked on into the big, squat chapel with its high pews, its carved pulpit, its organ.

She chose a seat at the back, then bowed her head to pray. She could think only of simple words with which to ask that Eleri Pritchard might yet rest peacefully and with her, the unhappy soul whose crying and singing haunted *Ty Mawr*. And she asked earnestly that Gareth's torment could be turned into happiness.

Mr Gruffydd, unfamiliar in a high-collared black suit, stepped up to the pulpit. His voice rang sonorously across the bowed heads of the congregation. Petra could understand nothing of what he said, but the language in which he said it, with its soft sibilants and subtle cadences, fascinated her.

The service was simple, but she sensed the meaning beneath it. There was something primitive and enduring in all of it, something that called out to something in her own nature that the valley had stirred into being.

The service ended with a hymn, sung loudly by a choir of well-scrubbed children who sat in rows on smaller chairs at the side, and as they came out, Mr Gruffydd, who was standing at the door wrapped in Sunday dignity, shook hands and chatted pleasantly.

"I came as I promised," Petra began as she reached him, but to her surprise, the smile died on his lips and his hand fell uneasily to his side.

"Good-morning, Miss Cunningham. I hope you enjoyed the service." His face showed acute embarrassment as he turned at once to speak in Welsh to the lady who stood behind her.

Petra stepped out into the yard feeling bewildered and thoroughly snubbed and was pleased to catch sight of Megan, her grey bun topped by a flowered hat, her ankle still bandaged.

"Megan! Good-morning! Are you better?"

Petra's voice died into an embarrassed whisper as Megan turned, gave her a long, unhappy look and then, tilting her square chin, walked past.

"Megan? Megan, what is it? What's wrong?"

Petra hurried after her but the way was barred by Myfi Chester. Myfi's eyes were fairly snapping and her cheeks quivered as she said,

"No use in making matters worse! Nobody likes to be made a fool of, you know, and Megan feels very bad about it all. Oh, I'm surprised you came to chapel this morning. I'd have thought you might have had the good sense to stay up at *Ty Mawr*, until you left!"

"Left? But I'm not – "

"Not leaving? Why do you go on pretending about it, Miss Cunningham? We all know now that you only came here to get the best price you could for the old place. But you should have been honest with us. You shouldn't have let us make you welcome, lead us to hope! That was a wicked thing to do. Yes, a very wicked thing to do. And that's all I've got to say, except that my brother will have the rents and the account books up to date when ever you want to collect them!"

"Myfi, wait! I don't know what you're talking about," Petra began, but Myfi Chester, still heaving with indignation, had marched ahead, the flowers on her hat bobbing in sympathy.

Petra stood bewildered, watching them all stream past her. It was senseless. Senseless! She had never seen such a change in people. They had been so friendly, so welcoming, and now it was all changed and for no reason she could understand. For a moment she considered walking across to the Post Office, hammering on the door and demanding an explanation. Then she changed her mind. It would probably be wiser to wait for a day or two until Myfi's temper had cooled. Then she would find out what had given them the idea she intended to leave.

Conscious of hostility in the sidelong glances cast at her by the groups of people who still stood around, Petra walked back to her car and stood in horror, for on the door, splashed in brilliant red paint, were the words, GO HOME JUDAS.

She stood aghast. For a moment her eyes stung with angry tears, then she got into the driving seat and accelerated down the street and out into open country.

When she reached *Ty Mawr*, she went to the kitchen and brought out rags and turpentine. The car would have to be cleaned and the rude, insulting message erased, but she doubted if she would ever be able to scrub the hurt from her mind.

It was mid-afternoon before the car was finished and her clothes were paint-stained and ruined. The car was reasonably presentable, but the door would probably need a respray, she thought despairingly. Perhaps, if she took it up to the garage, it would give her the opportunity to find out from Tommy what was going on, but for the time being, she contented herself with a final polish over the wings and bonnet. Then sighing unhappily, she went upstairs to wash herself and change her clothes.

Ty Mawr was pleasantly warm in contrast to the chilly damp outside. There was no feeling here of hostility, or threat. Petra luxuriated in a bath of hot, scented water, enjoying the draining away of tension. Whatever had happened to turn the people of the village against her would surely have some simple explanation. It had to have, for she could not settle here, she decided firmly, unless she was accepted. She had just dressed when the knocker banged hollowly against the front door.

Gareth Davies stood there and her first thought as she saw his broad, tall figure, was one of great thankfulness. No, it was more than that! She could no longer disguise from herself the knowledge that she was strongly attracted to him, that she was very close to falling in love with him, deeply in love.

"I was up at the village this morning," he began without preamble.

"And did you hear what happened? I can't understand it. I went to chapel and nobody would talk to me. Somebody painted my car up, too."

"Yes, that was Tommy Pritchard's girl. She did it while you were in chapel. Tommy isn't pleased about it, I hear. It was wrong of her, but she only expressed what everyone else is thinking."

"But why? *Why?*"

"Oh, for heaven's sake, don't play the innocent with me!" he exploded. "All that nonsense about hearing singing and crying. It was just an excuse so you could sell *Ty Mawr* with an easy conscience, wasn't it? The place made you afraid, so you couldn't keep it, eh, much as you wanted to? And I believed it! I was fool enough to worry about you!"

"But I *did* hear it! And Simon heard it too!"

"You can stand there and use his name as if it meant nothing to me!"

"To you?" she gasped. "What should Simon's name mean to *you*?"

"Nothing. Nothing at all, until I learned who owned it. Oh, you were clever to sneak him in and out of the village, but you were seen at Betws-y-Coed."

"That's not unlikely. We had coffee there and looked at the Falls."

"Wondering if you could get your itching hands on them, too! And I thought you reminded me of Eleri! I must have been blind. But not any more. Not any more, Judas girl!"

He turned abruptly and walked away, his long legs striding over the damp grass.

Petra bit on her lip until it hurt and clenched her fists. Something terrible had happened, something that was turning the new world she had found upside down. Welcome had become hostility and it all had something to do with Simon, something that they thought she already knew.

"But I shall stay," she muttered. "Nothing and nobody is going to drive me away. I'll not sell *Ty Mawr* and I'll *not* fall in love with Gareth Davies!"

But it was too late. As she went back into the big, empty house, she knew already that it was much too late Simon was a charming shadow in her mind, but Gareth was the substance of all her desiring.

The long, lonely evening stretched ahead. For the first time, Petra felt annoyance with Old Ifor for his refusal to have a telephone in the house. Over the phone, she could have spoken to Simon or to one of her girl-friends in

London, to anyone who was not part of this mist-hung valley. As it was, she was isolated from everything safe and familiar.

There was no sign of Moggy. Even the cat seemed to have deserted her. She put down some food for him and went through to the sitting-room, musing that she had not bothered to buy a newspaper since her arrival and it struck her that in the past few days, her world had shrunk into a narrow space of bewilderment and apprehension. And yet there had been such a friendly welcome for her in the beginning.

She jumped nervously. There was a tapping on the window beyond the curtain. It was probably only a branch, she told herself, but she could not recall any tree being so near the house. Then the tapping came again, urgent and insistent. Moving cautiously, she walked towards the window and drew back the curtain. Against the pane a white face pressed, its nose flattened against the glass, hair hanging lank about the hunched shoulders.

"Mother Carey!" Petra stepped back a pace. A skinny hand rapped the window again, sharply as if issuing a command.

"I'm coming, I'm coming!" She nodded encouragingly to the face beyond the glass and hurried out into the hall. As she pulled open the front door, the old woman shambled round the side of the house, her shawl fluttering in the breeze that blew across the river.

"What is it? What do you want?" Petra spoke anxiously, her eyes gentle.

An old hand reached out and fastened upon her arm with surprising strength and a torrent of words poured from the cracked old lips.

"Oh, I don't understand you," Petra gasped. "Please,

can't you say it in English?''

The old woman shook her head, pulling frantically at Petra's arm, the unfamiliar words still tumbling out. Only '*Eleri*' sounded clearly.

"But I'm *not* Eleri! Eleri is dead. Oh, please do try to understand.''

Petra raised her voice to no avail. The babbling and tugging continued, the gnarled hand jabbed in the direction of the trees.

"Do you want me to go with you somewhere?'' Petra demanded. "Is that it? Am I to go with you?''

The babbling ceased abruptly and Gwenny Carey, with an agility that belied her years, darted off into the gloom and was lost among the trees. Light swept an arc over the rough track and Petra stepped back hastily as a car halted beside the front door.

"Edward Bonner!'' Apprehension turned to relief and her greeting was much warmer than she had intended as the too-smooth, too-dapper figure uncoiled from the driving seat.

"Good-evening, Miss Cunningham. Nice to find you at home.''

His soft voice irritated her but at least she could understand what he said.

"The valley is hardly noted for its abundance of night-life,'' she retorted, crisply.

"Feeling a bit lonely, are you? I did try to tell you – ''

"Not in the least. In fact, I seem to be inundated with visitors at the moment,'' she interrupted.

"I see what you mean. That was old Mother Carey I saw, wasn't it?''

"Do you know her?'' Petra asked, surprised.

"Everybody knows her. I grew up in this valley, remember?''

"Of course." She hesitated for a moment then asked, "Would you like to come inside for a few minutes?"

"That's very kind of you, Miss Cunningham." He fell into step beside her as she turned back to the house. "A cup of coffee would be very nice. Talking to the old girl, were you?"

"I wouldn't exactly say that! She was talking *at* me. It was all in Welsh, you see, and I couldn't understand half a word of what she said."

"She's crazy." He said it as if it were an undisputed fact.

"She didn't seem to be crazy to me," Petra said, doubtfully. "She seemed to want to tell me something and then when your car came, she ran off. But I've a feeling it was important. I shall have to try to find her when morning comes and try to get to the bottom of it all."

"You'll have a job on," Bonner said, shrugging his padded shoulders. "She wanders around all over the place when the mood is on her, but I think she sleeps in a little place near the Cursing Well."

"You know about that, too?"

"Oh, yes. The local youngsters used to do their courting there in summer, out of sight of the chapel."

"I don't suppose you saw the cat on your way here?" Petra ventured. Quite suddenly she didn't want to talk to Bonner about the Cursing Well, or the strange red eye.

"Cat?" As Bonner held open the door, he raised his eyebrows in question.

"Old Ifor's big cat, Moggy. I've not seen him all day. Oh, well, he'll probably turn up when he's hungry."

Petra shrugged and went through to the kitchen with Bonner at her heels and while she made coffee, he lounged against the door, his pale, sharp eyes roving about the room.

"You know, my client might be induced to offer a little

more for the property," he said.

"Oh, no. Not that again, please." Petra set cups on a tray and measured coffee into them. "I'm not going to sell *Ty Mawr*. I won't sell, even if the entire village turns out with slings and arrows to drive me away!"

"The villagers want you to leave?"

"I don't know what anyone wants any more," she returned wearily. "I only know they welcomed me at first with open arms and then, when I went to chapel this morning, they treated me as if I had the plague."

"They're a funny lot," Bonner observed. "Very clannish. Let me carry the tray for you."

Petra relinquished it into his hands and followed him to the sitting-room. The parted curtains revealed a rectangle of darkness and moving to draw them close, Petra half-expected to see the ungainly figure of Mother Carey hovering beyond the glass, but there was only the quiet night.

"So what will you do?" Edward Bonner was asking.

"I'll stay here for another week and then I'll to back to London."

"So you *have* changed your mind?"

"To give my notice at work and pack up all my things. Then I'm coming back."

"And will you be married soon? I believe you mentioned a young man?"

"Simon."

She was silent, trying to conjure him in her mind. At last she said slowly, groping her way to the expressing of her conviction. "Simon has no – no reality here. He doesn't belong. He doesn't want to belong."

"And you think that you do?" He raised his eyebrows again.

"Not think, but know. I know that I belong – in spite of the villagers and the noises."

"What noises?"

"Oh, the noises in the night," she admitted reluctantly. "Last night in particular. I heard them quite plainly, but it doesn't frighten me now," she whispered, half to herself, "I'll not let a poor dead girl frighten me. I'm going to stay here, with or without Simon."

She stopped, catching her breath in a gasp as something heavy thudded against the window pane. Her eyes, wide and wary, sought Bonner's.

Edward Bonner rose to his feet, his face tense.

"Wait here. I'll see what's going on."

"Maybe it was a bird," Petra suggested. "A bird, flying against the window." She put down her cup and saucer, her hand shaking.

Bonner strode out of the room and, half fearful of staying behind alone, Petra followed him across the hall. At the door she hesitated, waiting, her fingers twisting nervously.

"Miss Cunningham." He had returned and his expression was one of sombre concern. In his arms something limp and black was cradled.

"Moggy? Oh, no!" She gazed in horror at the lolling, bloodstained head. "He's hurt?"

"He's dead," Bonner retorted. "No question of it. I'm very, very sorry. I don't think it was an accident, either."

"You mean somebody ..." She broke off, her lips dry, and stared at the poor, broken head. "Oh, to do that to a harmless old cat! Who could do such a thing?"

"I don't know, but whoever threw the poor beast against the window must have run off like the wind." He glanced down at the inert cat then said,

"Would you like me to – to get rid of him for you?"

"Will you, please?" She felt sick and knew she could not touch the poor, mangled body. "There's a cardboard box in the kitchen. Would you lay him in that for me?"

"Yes, of course." As he went down the passage Petra closed the front door, fearing even as she did so that eyes watched her out of the darkness.

"I really don't like to leave you here alone," Edward Bonner said, coming back into the hall. "Would you like to drive behind me, over to Betws-y-Coed and get a room there for the night? The tourist season hasn't started, yet, and there'll be bound to be somewhere you can stay."

It was a very tempting suggestion. Petra hesitated, then shook her head firmly.

"I'll stay here," she whispered. "I meant it when I said I'd not be driven out."

"Then you'll lock up and make sure the windows are secure?"

"I will. Goodnight, Mr Bonner, and thank you very much ..."

"And the offer I'm prepared to make for *Ty Mawr*?"

"Will be refused. I really mean it. *Ty Mawr* is not for sale."

He shrugged in mute resignation as she held the door open again.

She had closed it before his car roared down the drive and with the shutting of the door came the fierce, bright anger that cast out fear. To ignore her, to paint insults on her car, those were unpleasantnesses with which she could deal, but the killing of a defenceless animal defeated its own purpose. Petra was not frightened by it but coldly, bitterly angry. And that anger sustained her through the night, for she awoke in the morning with a new sense of purpose.

It was a fine day. Overhead, small fleecy clouds roamed a clear, high sky and the breeze carried the scent of growing things, yet by nightfall she knew it was possible that the mists would have descended again.

She pulled on slacks and sweater and drove away briskly. On the seat beside her was the cardboard box, with Moggy's old body resting beneath the lid. When she glanced at it, the anger bubbled up anew inside her and her hands tightened on the wheel.

She drew in a deep breath and eased her foot on the accelerator, slowing the car as she approached the steeply winding street. There was the bustle of Monday morning all around as she parked the car in the square. A large delivery van stood outside the post office and the garage forecourt was busy with cars. A bus, packed with schoolchildren, went slowly past on the main road.

Petra picked up the box, its weight an obscenity in her arms and went into the post office. There were several women there, clutching shopping baskets, scarves over their heads. Their cheerful conversation died away as the door-bell tinkled her arrival and Petra felt the wave of hostility that flowed out to meet her. Behind the counter, Myfi Chester stiffened visibly.

Petra walked up to her, her back stiff with indignation, and setting the box down with a little thump said,

"I've brought something to show you. It was left for me yesterday and I'm sure you'll all know who was responsible. Go on – open it and take a good, long look."

Myfi Chester shot a puzzled glance then slowly lifted the lid. There was a silence, then one of the others who had crowded around gave a loud, horrified gasp.

"It's Old Ifor's cat," Petra said, tightly. "You remember Moggy, don't you? He was a pretty old cat, but I think he had the right to die in his own time. I don't think he deserved to have that done to him."

"But this is awful," Myfi stammered. Her face paled and she shivered as she looked down into the box. "Who could have done such a terrible thing?"

"You tell *me!*" Petra flung. "But whoever it was obviously meant to frighten me away. Like the paint on my car and the voices singing and laughing and crying. Well, it won't work! I'm here to stay. I'll not accept any offers from anybody's clients and I'll not leave! I'll not leave for any reason at all and so you can tell that to whoever did *this!*"

"Miss Cunningham! Wait!" Myfi put up her hand in a pleading gesture, but Petra spun round on her heel and strode out, banging the door behind her so that the little bell above it vibrated madly.

"I don't care," she fumed, warming to the wrath inside her, slamming the car shut. "They can do what they want. I'll go when I'm good and ready and not one minute before!"

She released the brake and let out the clutch fiercely and the little car jerked forward, rear wheels spinning. She drove furiously and when she reached *Ty Mawr*, anger still burned white-hot within her. She jerked to a halt and sat for a while, taking deep, unsteady breaths. She was being silly. Anger was a wasted emotion.

She looked around her at the silent mountains, the tender green of the trees, the swathes of bluebells and narcissi. Anger was an intrusion in this lovely place.

She sighed, calmer now. A cup of tea, that was what she needed. A cup of strong, sweet tea and a good, hard think.

There were marks on the step. Chalk marks. She stared down at them, puzzled. An eye with a pupil circled in it, a rough outline of a figure and the name 'Eleri', tailing into a squiggle.

Someone has been to see me, Petra thought, gazing around her. Someone had been and, finding her out, had left a message. That person could have only been Mother Carey. The eye obviously referred to the Cursing Well, the figure presumably was herself and the name Eleri could only refer to the dead girl. The old woman wanted to tell her something, that Petra knew. Perhaps, now, she had realised at last that the newcomer at *Ty Mawr* was not Eleri returned.

Petra ran back to her car and drove away, spurred by an urgency she could not fully understand, knowing only that she must get to the quarry, and quickly, if she was ever to solve the mystery of Eleri's death and set free for all time, Gareth Davies' tormented heart.

Ten

The sun shone brightly as Petra swung onto the side road that wound up to the old quarry, and then she was climbing steadily to the rim of the tumbled slate.

Before her lay a steep path littered with boulders and smaller stones that led downwards, curving about the quarry face like a crooked old finger. Grey dust swirled about her ankles as she left the car and began the slow descent by a path that here and there lost itself in sharp ridges of slate and clumps of moss.

The well was almost at the bottom of the sloping sides of the quarry. There were rusted tracks laid along the level ground and a rusted chain clanked as it swung stiffly in the wind against an overhang of rock. A rook cawed harshly above her, but there was no other sign of life.

The well was dry. She leaned her palms on its wide rim and looked down into its depths. There was nothing there but dried-up mud, scattered with flints and pebbles. On the stone edge of the well, names and entwined hearts were scored deeply, some almost obliterated by time, and on the overhanging rock was painted in red, the eye she had seen in Eleri's picture – the same eye that was chalked on the front step of *Ty Mawr*.

A little shower of stones bounced past her. She looked up

sharply and saw someone moving along the rim of the quarry. The sun was shining in her eyes, but Petra recognised the scrawny figure with its flapping shawl. There was a flash of sunlight on windscreen and the screech of tyres and then the ungainly figure was falling with outstretched arms down the face of the quarry. On the crest of the high ridge, a car engine raced briefly, then all was quiet.

It had all happened so quickly that it was over before Petra had registered the event in her conscious mind. And with the realisation came shock. Mother Carey had been forced over the top of the quarry, deliberately forced.

She shuddered, her teeth clamping down on her lip to stifle a scream of fear. The old woman had been on her way to the Cursing Well, but she had been prevented, savagely and wantonly prevented.

Petra stumbled across the rusted tracks and stared up at the misshapen figure sprawled in the branches of a bush, ten feet below the overhanging rim of the quarry. The body was still and limp, like that of a broken doll. Dust was rising around the tumbled shawl.

"I must get help. I must tell someone," Petra jerked aloud.

Her voice echoed back hollowly. Shading her eyes, she looked up again to where her own car was still parked and heard the faint whine of an engine. The car was returning and her first impulse was to shout and wave her arms, but the impulse died as she realised that whoever had sent Mother Carey over the edge had probably returned to rid themselves of a witness. If she were to scramble back up the path towards her own car, someone might well be waiting.

She shrank back into the shadow of the overhanging rock. Whoever waited would know she was down here, still and in a little while, if she did not show herself, would be only too likely to come down in search of her. So her only hope, she conceded dully, was to climb up the other side of the quarry and work her way round to *Ty Mawr* on foot. It would take a long time, but with any luck she would be able to continue past *Ty Mawr* and on to the next valley, where Gareth lived. Gareth would know what to do. He would help her, even if he despised her as a Judas girl.

Carefully, lest the rolling of a stone should betray her presence, Petra edged along to the sheer face, looking upwards for some sign of a path.

The floor of the quarry narrowed to a point and a chimney of rock snaked up to the main road again. There were staples set in the rock and projections of slate that offered handholds, but she had no means of testing how secure they were. And the top of the quarry was frighteningly high above her head.

Cautiously, she set her foot on an iron staple, took a deep breath and began to climb. She forced herself to move slowly, to keep her eyes firmly on the rock face, to lean inwards from time to time while her pounding heart steadied. Once, her foot slipped and she hung helpless for an instant, blind with fear, not daring to think of the drop below her. Then her groping foot found the staple again and she pulled herself up to the next projecting ledge. Her hands were cut and bleeding by the time she reached the treacherous grass-grown verge, and perspiration ran down into her eyes.

One final effort and she lay by the side of the road, her breath emerging in painful gasps, tears of mingled terror and relief running unchecked down her cheeks. After a few moments she cautiously raised her head. Sunshine glinted on the roof of her own car, but another vehicle was parked further down the road, just on the bend. It was too far away to be identified positively, and there was no sign of anyone around, but she dared not risk going back. Instead, she wriggled cautiously into a sitting position, pulled off her shoes, and with one brief glance down the road, scrambled to her feet and walked quickly away.

The small stones hurt her feet and she winced, terrified as she went that running feet might gain on her from behind. At the first bend in the road she paused to put on her shoes again and then went briskly on, moving as swiftly as her still-trembling legs would carry her.

The road curved down towards *Ty Mawr*. She could see its roof below her like the roof of a toy house. Despite her fatigue and the heat of the sun shining down on her uncovered head, she began to run, stumbling down the narrow track that led into the valley. At its foot she hesitated, catching her gasping breath as she looked to left and right over the quiet meadows.

One way lay the steep village street and chapel-dominated square; the other led to the old house that stood foursquare against a background of slate and granite peaks that marked the high ridge-road. It was possible that the villagers would offer her no help at all, even if she could convince them of what had happened to the old woman. Better to go straight to *Ty Mawr*, change her flimsy shoes, then set off again to Gareth's farm, hoping she might pass a telephone kiosk on the way. The very thought of Gareth gave her a new courage as she forced herself onward, the river rippling silver as she hurried up the broad drive.

Her optimism faded as she reached the front steps. The door of *Ty Mawr* was closed and her handbag, which held the key, was still in her abandoned car.

Petra sat down heavily on the steps and buried her face in

her hands. She should have gone to the village. She should have bitten back her pride and asked the villagers for help, thrust upon them the responsibility of taking care of one of their own.

She ran her tongue round her dry, cracked lips. She was hot and thirsty and so tired that her very bones seemed to ache and throb. And she was desperately afraid, for danger still danced all around her. She could feel it like a presence in the air. Mother Carey had wanted to tell her something and it seemed beyond all doubt, that the frail old woman had been forced over the edge of the quarry to an awful death. Eleri had drawn a picture of the dark water and met her own end there.

But it was useless to sit here and speculate while the danger came closer. She lifted her head and turning, gave the door behind her a half-hopeless push. There was a faint click as it yielded. She gasped. It was unbelievable, but she could only assume she had neglected to fasten it properly when she had first set out. Surely that was an omen, a good omen?

Stepping thankfully into the cool, slate-floored hall her relief lived shortly. Dear God, please not again? No more – please, *please*, no more?

But the house was filled with laughter, sweet, high, childish laughter, that shivered up to the gallery and gathered like an echo in the high, tall beams of the ceiling. It beat all about her and assaulted her ears, her eyes, the very air she breathed. Behind her the door was wide open and Petra knew that all she had to do was turn and flee to safety and sanity, but she knew, too, that if she went now, she would never again return to *Ty Mawr*. Now was the time to stand firm in defence of her beloved old house. She dare not hesitate. Shaking with naked terror, her nails

digging into her scratched and grimy palms, she followed
the sound to its source, like one who walks in a trance.

The laughing grew louder as she walked down the
passage, the child's voice gay and light. It was beginning to
erupt into a cascade of words,

One, two, three, Eleri,

a song that should have been endearing, but instead chilled
her to the marrow of her bones. And Mother Carey was
dead, at the quarry.

The door of the sitting-room was wide open and the voice
was so clear, so real, that Petra had a sudden, appalling
picture of a dripping corpse, weeds clinging to its skeletal
fingers.

Stop it, urged the voice of her failing reason. Stop it! The
dead can't return. They don't sing or laugh!

Her legs were useless, her mouth dry and she let go a sob
that vibrated with primitive fear. Her heart thudded loudly
in her ears and she wanted to surrender to the blackness
that swirled around her. Blindly, she stumbled forward,
swaying from side to side, arms outstretched in a last,
desperate plea for help.

Then hands grasped her shoulders, steadied her, pulled
her back from the oblivion that called her. She forced open
her eyes and looked into Simon's face.

"All right," he whispered, drawing her close to him. "It's
all right ..."

"Simon! Oh, Simon!" was all she could gasp before the
tears came; hot, stinging tears of blessed relief.

He held her until her shaking body was still, making little
hushing noises, pulling her cheek close to his.

"There. There now. You're safe, quite safe."

But she would never be safe again, she thought wildly.
Not until the singing stopped, not until the laughter was

stilled. She drew back from his arms and spoke imploringly.

"You can hear it, can't you? *Can't you*, Simon?"

"Yes," he said, softly. "I can hear it."

Her head jerked upwards. If he could hear it, then why was he so calm, so unafraid? How could he bear to listen to it? She wanted to reason with him, but no words would come so she laid her head on his shoulder again as the laughing filled the room, cascading from the ceiling, the walls, ringing inside her head, obliterating all thought and reason.

Simon was speaking, his words urgent in her ear. Petra squeezed shut her eyes, concentrating hard.

"... a tape recording," he was saying, "Darling, that's all it is."

"A *tape* ...?"

"Never heard of them?" he nodded. There was a faint, amused smile on his lips. "You play them back on little machines. Just the flick of a switch, that's all it takes."

The flick of a switch, she thought dully, then searching inside her muddled brain she whispered,

"Then who was flicking the switches, Simon? Tell me that, will you?"

"Easy." His smile was suddenly maddening. "It was all rigged up to certain of the light switches. There was one in the master bedroom, one in the – "

"But why? And where's the *little machine*?" she mimicked, anger replacing fear.

"In the junk room. Didn't you find it?"

The long, light room, her mind supplied. The room with the wide, blue-tiled hearth, where children should play.

"But the singing, the laughing? The sound of it is everywhere ..."

"And your uncle was a hi-fi addict. He has speakers

everywhere, carefully placed, well hidden."

He smiled, as if it were all so simple. And come to think of it, Petra acknowledged, she had seen some equipment in the junk room, but it hadn't registered.

"How do you know all this, Simon? How did you find it all out?" Suddenly she felt a dart of suspicion. "And what are you doing here? You were going to London. I left you at Betws-y-Coed."

"And now I'm back again."

He turned abruptly and left the room and immediately the laughing stopped.

"There you are. Flick the switch again and it stops. Is there no end to the miracles of modern science?" His voice was faintly mocking and unease jabbed through her again. But there was no time for questions and accusations. She remembered again the frail old body, huddled against the quarry-face, and the horror was back again.

"A phone, Simon. You've got to get me to a phone! It's Mother Carey. They did it deliberately! She's dead, I think, but I must get an ambulance and the police. Where is your car, Simon?"

Suddenly she stopped. The car at the quarry! Dear God, no!

"*Your* car?" Her lips mouthed the words. "It was *you*?"

Her eyes opened wide with terror and the smell of fear filled her nostrils like acrid smoke. The room was spinning again but she grasped the back of a chair and willed herself to be calm.

"No, Petra. My car is round the back. It's been there for the last hour."

"Then it was Bonner!" she gasped. "His car is like yours! Oh, Simon, please hurry! *Please*?"

But he stood his ground and said, impassively,

"There's no need. The ambulance has been sent for – and the police."

"But *who* sent for them? Who told you? How do you know all this?"

"Because I was there, Petra." His voice was completely without emotion. "I was there. With Edward Bonner."

"There? With *Bonner*?" Fear touched her again. "You watched him force her over the edge?"

"Don't be so stupid. Nobody was forced anywhere. It was an accident. Suddenly, from out of nowhere, she was under the car wheels ..."

"I don't believe you," she flung. "You drove away, and then you came back, to look for me – to make sure I didn't – "

She backed towards the door, her eyes wide with terror.

"Little fool!" Grasping her wrist, he pulled her to him. "We didn't even know you were there, you, or the old woman. And it *was* an accident."

"You drove away, left her ..."

"We went to phone for an ambulance. Then Bonner went back to wait until it came. I give you my word, Petra, nobody tried to harm the old girl. It was an accident and you'll never prove otherwise!" He looked directly into her eyes. "And as for coming back to look for you – well, that's just plain crazy. What do you think we are, then? A couple of gangsters?"

"Then tell me what you were doing at the quarry?" she spat. "You knew I would be at the Cursing Well. The eye was chalked on the step for anybody to see."

She stopped, breathless, waiting for his reply, willing herself to be brave.

"Well, Simon?"

He sighed and took out his cigarette case. His hands, she

noticed, were steady as he flicked his lighter and lit a cigarette.

"Sorry, darling, but I went to the quarry for quite a different reason. I certainly didn't know you would be there. If I had, I wouldn't have – "

He stopped suddenly, then shrugged his shoulders as though he knew he had said too much and must convey the impression that he didn't care.

"You wouldn't have gone, is that it, Simon?" Petra finished, flatly. "I can well understand that, considering the lengths you went to, to convince me you had gone back to London."

He drew on his cigarette then released the smoke in little puffs, watching them languidly as they floated upwards. Then he looked at her blankly, his lips clasped tight and in that moment, any lingering doubts she might have had vanished, and Petra knew she had never loved him.

"Well," she whispered. "Am I not to be given any explanation at all? Oh, I realise I was really fooled with the tape recordings. My uncle must have made them a long time ago. Maybe he was fond of Eleri and wanted to hear her voice. Maybe he liked tinkering with gadgets, but who knew about those tapes? Certainly not Megan, or she would have warned me. And Gareth Davies didn't know, either, I'm sure of that. But *you* knew, Simon. You switched it on today, didn't you? Why did you do it? To frighten me into leaving *Ty Mawr*? Is that it?"

"Heaven knows," he shrugged. "I don't know why you came here in the first place and why you should want to stay on when you are ignored and insulted – "

"What do you mean, ignored and insulted? How did you know about that? And how did you get into the house, anyway? The front door was locked. I *know* it was locked."

"So many questions, Petra. You're getting as suspicious as the locals."

"And *they* didn't get suspicious until after they had seen me with you. They were all right, and then you came and since then there's been nothing but trouble."

She shook her head angrily. Now, all her fear was gone. She was sure, beyond all doubt, that someone had tried to frighten her away and suddenly she was determined to know who and why.

"I can understand that for some reason Uncle Ifor wanted to hear Eleri singing, but he wouldn't have made a tape of her crying, and I heard her crying too, Simon."

"Oh, for pity's sake, tell her. We'll get no peace until she knows."

Petra flung round. Edward Bonner stood in the doorway, his eyes amused, his mouth a thin line of anger, and she had the uncanny sensation of looking at two persons within one body; the one urbane and sophisticated, the other coldly savage.

"That crying tape wasn't Eleri Pritchard. Your boyfriend managed to get one made, then rigged it up while you were asleep, the other night," Edward Bonner smiled, his voice soft, too soft. "You'd already been frightened by the singing, so he came prepared to capitalise upon that. Oh, we knew there were tapes that were wired-up to the light switches, Eleri told me about them."

"Eleri? You knew Eleri?"

"Old Ifor was a great one for secrets. He was for ever playing about with tapes and things, but he was afraid people might think it a bit childish, so he made Eleri promise not to tell. Thick as thieves those two were ..."

"But Eleri told you?"

"She told me everything," Bonner smirked. "All that last

summer when she was engaged to Gareth Davies, she would sneak away to the Cursing Well and we'd meet there. She had a wild streak in her did Eleri, and a taste for gaiety. I used to tell her about city life and the fun she'd be missing if she married Davies and rusticated on a farm."

"Eleri and *you*?" Petra stared at him, trying to make sense of his words.

"And what's so strange about that? She wasn't in love with Gareth Davies. She was only marrying him to please the old man. Oh, she was fond of him, but I was more exciting, see?"

"Then why didn't she marry you? Surely my uncle didn't have all that much influence over her?"

"Ah, but money talks, doesn't it? Eleri thought she was going to inherit *Ty Mawr*. A sad shock it was when she found out that blood is thicker than water and an unknown great-niece was going to get it."

"And when she told you that, you dropped her!"

"Oh, no. I'd never have married her. Do you think I'd tie myself down to a valley girl? No, I made it plain to her the last time we met that a bit of fun was one thing, but marriage is something else again."

"So she drowned herself? Because of you, she drowned herself!"

Looking at him, Petra thought it incredible.

"Ah, but they *said* it was an accident," he shrugged. "Nobody had any proof about – anything ..."

But Eleri gave the doll and her drawings to Mother Carey, and Mother Carey had tried to see me, Petra reasoned, tried to tell me something.

"You were on the cliff road just now," she said slowly, "and I still think you forced Mother Carey over the edge of the quarry. Then you waited, knowing I was down there – "

"It was an *accident*," Bonner said doggedly, "so you can think what you like. And for your information, when they got the old woman into the ambulance about fifteen minutes ago, she was still alive. I waited there, you see, until they got her up. Not the action of a guilty man, eh, Miss Cunningham? And there's a fair chance she'll pull through, the doctor said. So go and tell the police what you think, if that's what you want to do. You'll look silly, won't you, when the old girl confirms what I have told you."

"What he says is the truth, Petra," Simon urged. "You had been frightened and upset and naturally you were ready to think the worst. Nobody tried to harm the old woman and nobody wanted to harm you. Do you honestly think I would have agreed to murder — because that's what it would have been."

"Agreed?" She swung round on him. "*Agreed?* What have you to do with all this?"

There was a little silence while the two men glanced at each other, then Simon said,

"I wanted to persuade you to marry me, that's all."

"And sell *Ty Mawr*? What profit would the sale of *Ty Mawr* have brought you?"

"My, but she's a bright girl," Bonner approved.

"Oh, no. I've a feeling I've been anything but bright," Petra flung. "Who *really* wants to buy the land? Not some retired Colonel, I'll bet!"

"A city-based development company," Simon supplied with a gesture of resignation. "They've been interested in the property for the last couple of years. The entire valley can be developed as a winter sports centre, with a Lido for the summer months. It would be easy enough to flood the valley ..."

"Flood the valley? But the villagers would hate it!"

"The villagers are a stupid lot, a hundred years behind the times," Bonner interjected. "They don't know when they're on to a good thing."

"But the character of the place would be ruined. It would all be spoiled. And *Ty Mawr* would disappear completely."

"She's bright, too. Bright and sentimental," Bonner sneered.

"It sounds vulgar and garish," Petra answered, coldly.

"That was what the old man said," Simon shrugged.

"You knew my uncle?"

"I met him on two occasions. I came up to try to talk him into selling. I've been hired, you see, to look after the publicity for the Centre. There's a damn good rake-off for me if I can pull it off."

"But Uncle Ifor refused – and then you met me – was that why you got to know me? Was that why you asked me to marry you? *Was it?*"

"Let's just say that I don't give up easily where money is concerned," he smiled cruelly.

"So you teamed up with Bonner, here? Oh, now I know why the village suddenly turned against me, after they'd seen me with you! They knew all about your scheme for the valley!"

"There were rumours. There are always rumours," Bonner supplied. "They wanted to keep word of the proposed deal from you, I suppose."

"But there isn't going to be any deal," Petra ground. "I said I intended to live here and nothing has changed. I won't sell!"

"I can see we'll have to persuade her," Bonner whispered, smiling a little.

"No! I want none of that! There'll be no violence," Simon jerked. "The cat was bad enough. Just give up,

Bonner, admit defeat – "

"The cat? You killed Moggy?" Petra's mouth dried with horror.

"That's right. I did it. Ran over it. Your boyfriend merely obliged by throwing it against the window," Bonner smirked.

Nauseated, Petra flung round.

"So you never intended to go back to London, Simon? You stayed, to help frighten me into selling." She felt sick and cold.

"And the villagers helped out too, all unwittingly," Bonner supplied, laughing mirthlessly. "Because, having seen the two of us together, they jumped to the conclusion that you were going to sell out."

"Well, they were wrong. I won't sell and you had both better go – *now*! And if I ever see you on *Ty Mawr* land again, Bonner, I'll have you thrown off!" Then quietly she turned to face the man she might so easily have married. "As for you, Simon, thank heaven I found you out in time. I hope, one day, you'll find the rich heiress you are looking for, and when you do, I hope she gives you hell!"

Pushing past them, she walked angrily into the hall and held wide the front door. Unspeaking, they walked past her, then Bonner turned and held his hand towards her.

"Here you are, Miss Cunningham. It fits the back door."

"Where did you get this?" Petra demanded, staring down at the old-fashioned key in her hand.

"Eleri gave it to me, ages ago. She often slept here, you know," he smiled. "Like I said, Eleri had a wild streak in her ..."

"Why – you!" Petra jerked, raising her hand as if to strike him. The thought of the man letting himself into *Ty Mawr*, creeping along the corridors in the darkness to

Eleri's room was a sickening one. She drew in a deep breath and her hand fell limply to her side. He wasn't worth her contempt. He simply wasn't worth it.

"Get out!" she hissed. "Get *out!*"

"Oh, I'm going, Miss Cunningham," he said, quietly, "but first let me wish you well of your big, old, empty house. Wait until the novelty wears off. Wait until the winter, when you'll be snowed up for weeks on end. It can be lonely, in the valley, oh, very lonely. And you'll never be quite sure, will you? Every man you meet you'll wonder. Is it you he wants, or *Ty Mawr?*"

He laughed and turned on his heel. He was still laughing as he banged shut the door of his car.

Petra closed the door behind her. She didn't want to say goodbye to Simon. She didn't want ever to see him again. He'd made a fool of her and –

She straightened her shoulders and marched defiantly into the kitchen, the tap-tap of her heels echoing loudly in her ears.

Slowly she filled the kettle then switched it on to boil. She looked down at the large, empty saucer at her feet. Even Moggy had gone. Bonner was right. Suddenly the future seemed to stretch ahead of her, empty and lonely.

A tear ran down her nose and plopped onto her hand and she let it lie there.

Eleven

Petra sat, drained of all feeling, her hands still unwashed her clothes soiled, one trouser knee torn beyond repair. Without emotion she regarded her fingernails, tips torn and broken, the carefully applied enamel chipped away.

A cloud drifted over the afternoon sun and without moving her head she glanced through the window at the darkening sky. A rainstorm threatened and she shivered. Tempestuous April. Soft, mild days and sudden squalls.

She struck a match and held it to the kindling in the hearth. Fascinated, she watched the flames lick around the wood-chips then dance on the copper coal-scuttle. It reminded her of the first time she had seen the room – was it only a week ago – and pictured firelight and children and a Christmas tree. There was laughter there and love and Gareth Davies' image had intruded. Gareth, with whom she had fallen deeply and inexplicably in love. Gareth, bound to Eleri, whose wraith arose from the dark water to torment him.

With cold detachment Petra thought instead of Simon. Simon had never loved her. Deliberately he had sought her out because she was necessary to his schemes. He had learned, that day he met Ifor Jones, that *Ty Mawr* was to be left to a great-niece whom the old man had never met.

Edward Bonner learned of it, too. Eleri had told him, and from that moment on his interest in her ceased. Had Eleri imagined herself to be in love with Bonner, Petra mused. Could the love she felt for Gareth have died so quickly?

But my love for Simon died like the blowing out of a candle flame, Petra reasoned. Their meeting was so romantic. The party was crowded and noisy and she had dropped her purse.

"You must be Petra," said a voice and she looked up into incredibly blue eyes.

"I'm Simon." He squatted beside her, handing back the lipstick that had rolled across the floor. Then helping her to her feet and taking her elbow, he guided her to the buffet.

"White wine, isn't it?" he smiled as bemused she nodded her head. "Now, let me see ..." Carefully he filled a plate for her. "Nothing fishy and you don't like olives. I know so much about you, you see."

He knew, too, that she liked Shakespeare and the next evening they watched Romeo and Juliet, then walked along the Embankment, fingers entwined, and saw the September sky sprinkle the river with stars.

"Marry me, Petra?"

He asked the question so often and Penny and Iris demanded to know what was holding her back, and didn't she realise that men who proposed marriage didn't grow on trees?

Simon did his homework well and I fell for it, Petra thought, dully. But a small voice of reason had nagged constantly inside her head and she had heeded it. She loved him, she had thought, but there were no stars in her eyes, no delirious highs, no abysmal lows. She never felt dizzy with happiness just to think of him or sick with fear when he did not call her. She had never ached for the nearness of his body, or the touch of his hands on her thighs, her breasts.

And then she came to *Ty Mawr* and there was Gareth who called her a foreigner and gave her warm woolly socks and wellington boots that didn't fit. Gareth, who belonged to Eleri who had died, rather than marry him. And the wound went deep, for although the heartache had diminished, the hurt to his pride remained. Gareth Davies would never let himself love again until the shadow of the dark water was banished. And when would that be, Petra mused. How long before he was free?

She leaned over and arranged more logs on the fire. The corners of the room were gloomy, now, and rain had begun to spatter the window panes.

Why had Eleri done it? Mutely Petra asked the question of the flickering flames. Eleri had been a sweet girl, a chapel-going girl, Gareth said.

But that wasn't wholly true, for there was another Eleri, a girl who could leave the arms of the man she was about to marry and creep to the Cursing Well, a girl who gave the key to *Ty Mawr* to her lover. Then she became another creature.

'*Oh, she had a wild streak in her, did Eleri, and a taste for gaiety ...*'

Petra closed her eyes and shuddered as she recalled the blatant insinuation in Bonner's voice. What had it been like, at the quarry? Did they make promises beneath the unseeing red eye? Did they make secrets beside that lonely well – secrets that showed in the eyes of a nineteen year old girl?

The clock ticked slowly, loudly. The house was empty and dark, but Petra was no longer afraid. She had convinced herself that *Ty Mawr* was haunted by Eleri's wraith, but there had been a simple explanation and the flicking of a switch silenced it for all time. No more singing. No more laughter. Go back, Eleri, to the dark water and take your secrets with you.

Urgently Petra jumped to her feet. Now the blind terror of the morning was receding and in its place came anger.

"Fool, Petra Cunningham! Blind little fool!"

She said the words loudly to the empty room. All the unspeakable fear, the blood-chilling horror – Simon had caused them. And when he heard it, when Eleri's laughter echoed through the house, Simon had feigned unease, comforted her, sat beside her as she fell into a drugged sleep. What an accomplished actor he was.

She wiped her hand across her lips as if to rub away his kisses. His betrayal was complete yet his conscience sat easy, still, on his shoulder.

"Oh, Eleri," she whispered. "You suffered, too."

Eleri had felt the pain of betrayal when Bonner denied their love and Gareth felt pain, too, as the cold, limp body of a girl he thought he knew was lifted from the still, malevolent water.

"Eleri," she whispered again. "Poor little Eleri. Poor, proud Gareth ..."

A wave of sympathy washed over Petra and she tilted her head, alert once more and in command of her senses. Nothing would be gained by brooding. Simon was a heel, but unlike Eleri, she had found out in time.

"Count your blessings girl," she whispered grimly as she mounted the stairs, two at a time. She needed a hot bath, a change of clothing and time to think. And when she had soaked the pain from her screaming muscles and scrubbed the memory of that panic-ridden climb from her torn and grimy hands, she would find a telephone and ask the hospital for news of old Gwenny Carey. And Megan – she must see Megan. There were things to be said, misunderstandings to be righted, a doll to be given back. The doll was Megan's, by rights.

Suddenly Petra stopped dead in her tracks. She couldn't give it back, not yet. Eleri's doll held the key to the mystery, she knew it. The blank eyes of Eleri's doll held secrets, too.

A hot soak in the silk-soft water had quickly revived Petra and she sat snug in fresh slacks and sweater, watching the flickering firelight, listening to the crackle and hiss of blazing apple logs in the stone hearth.

It was strange, she mused, that up until now, she had never given serious thought to the financial side of *Ty Mawr*. That she wanted to live in the rambling old house was without question. That she loved the soaring peaks, the river-valley, the people around her had long ago been established. When her uncle's affairs were finally settled, she supposed, there would be several thousand pounds to invest and that, coupled with the income from the cottages, would cover the upkeep of *Ty Mawr* and feed and clothe her. But most of the land was idle and that was morally wrong, as well as being highly unprofitable.

Gareth would know what was best to be done, she mused. Gareth wrested a living from the stony, ungenerous hill pastures that surrounded *Ty Coch* and it was a challenge to him, a constant battle with the elements and one he had to win. Could she, Petra wondered, bring the gardens to production again, repair the greenhouses and learn to grow salad crops? Or might she get help from the village and turn *Ty Mawr* into a guest house? Simon and Bonner had gone to unbelievable lengths to drive her from the valley. They knew the value of its peace and beauty; might not others recognise it, too?

Petra dismissed the idea with a shrug of her shoulders. No one in the village would come now, to *Ty Mawr*. They had ignored her and snubbed her, demanded that she go. The hand of welcome had been withdrawn and now, too late, she knew why.

She clucked impatiently and scrambled to her feet. A wind was blowing down from the mountains, flinging rain against the windows. Outside, a grey twilight hovered and Petra drew the curtains then moved round the room, switching on the lamps one by one. She might, she supposed, watch television, but she shrugged away the thought. Perhaps she could search through Uncle Ifor's records and tapes and find some music to suit her mood? But she had had enough of the old man's gadgets for a little while, she decided with grim humour. There was, of course, the kitchen. Maybe her restlessness was caused by an empty stomach? How long since she had eaten? But eating alone was no fun. Later, perhaps, she would open a tin of soup, make some sandwiches ...

Suddenly, as if she knew she could delude herself no longer, she gave an exasperated cry.

"Face it," she whispered, tight-lipped, "it isn't going to work out. *Ty Mawr* isn't for you, Petra. *Ty Mawr* is a house to live in and love in and raise children in. And the land needs a man to master it and, oh – "

Tears pricked her eyes and in that instant all the tension and fear of the past week burst about her and the memory of her fearsome flight from the quarry rushed back with a clarity that was all too real. She covered her face with hands that trembled and gave way to weeping. She wept for a dream that had died, for Simon's treachery, for Eleri who had carried secrets to her death, and for Gareth. But mostly she cried for her own loneliness. *Ty Mawr* was useless to her unless she could share it with someone and that someone was Gareth Davies. But Gareth had looked at her with contempt and called her Judas girl, and anyway, she conceded sadly, Gareth would always belong to Eleri.

"Dear God, I'm so unhappy," she choked and the tears came afresh, hotter and more bitter as she cried for the safeness of Gareth's arms about her and the feel of his mouth on hers and a love that would never be.

The clock on the mantelshelf began to chime, its tones high and sweet and Petra glanced up, startled, to find that its fingers pointed to seven o'clock. She blew her nose vigorously and dabbed at her eyes. She had so much to be grateful for, she told herself ashamedly. Why, she might now be lying in hospital like poor Mother Carey, ill and friendless and alone.

Impulsively, she jumped to her feet. She would telephone the hospital, now. There was no need for her to go down to the village – there was a phonebox somewhere along the Betws-y-Coed road. It was the least she could do, and in a strange way, she felt she owed something to the ragged old creature who was once Eleri's friend.

Shrugging into her coat, she slammed the front door behind her, glad to be doing something to help quell the black depression that had taken hold of her. Dubiously, she told herself that it was a reaction to the events of the morning, but deep inside herself she knew it was something more. She was being forced to face facts, to look at the situation clearly and sensibly and acknowledge that she could not, would not, live alone at *Ty Mawr*.

"I'll worry about it tomorrow," she whispered. "In the morning, I shall feel better." And there would be no singing tonight, no laughing, to strike terror into the marrow of her bones. The voices had gone and it was a comforting thought. She would find a telephone then return to the quarry to retrieve her car. The long walk would do her good and she was not afraid of the darkness. After what had happened since she came to *Ty Mawr*, Petra thought grimly, she was certain that nothing would ever make her afraid again.

She pulled up her coat collar then, hands deep in pockets, head down, she walked quickly into the dark, wind-tossed night.

Once she found a telephone kiosk, Petra had little trouble in getting through to the sister-in-charge of the ward in which Mother Carey lay.

"She is resting comfortably. Her condition is satisfactory," she was told.

"But is she conscious?" Suddenly it mattered a great deal to Petra that the strange old recluse should get better. "When last I saw her she was – well, I thought she was dead."

"She was very lucky. Very, very lucky." The ward-sister warmed to the anxiety in Petra's voice. "A little miracle, I suppose you could call it."

"And is she badly injured?"

"No, nothing too serious. A fractured wrist and bruises and abrasions. She's old, of course, and frail. Sometimes, with old people, shock can do more harm than injuries."

"But hasn't she told you anything? Didn't she say how she got there?"

"No. No, she didn't."

"Then how do you know what happened?"

"As far as I know, a man saw it all. It was he who phoned for the ambulance and the police."

"The police?" Edward Bonner had told the *police* about it?

"That's right. Look – who are you?" The friendly Celtic

voice became suddenly wary. "Are you a friend of Miss Carey's? According to the local constable, she has always been a bit of a – well, a hermit, so to speak."

"Yes, I think she was," Petra replied cautiously. "I think she lived a bit – rough."

"Indeed. So it's maybe all for the best." The sister's tone was brisk, now. "Once we have her fit, we shan't let her go back to her old ways. She'll be well looked after at the Rest Home. *Did* you say you knew her, Miss – "

"Cunningham," Petra supplied, "and I did know her. But we couldn't talk, you see. I have no Welsh, and she has no English. I think originally she mistook me for someone else."

"I see. And did you say you had actually seen the accident, Miss Cunningham?"

"Why, yes. But didn't Mother – *Miss* Carey tell you about it?"

"No, I'm afraid she didn't. Miss Carey isn't very coherent at the best of times, it seems, so it's hardly likely she could have told us very much about it, even had she been able to remember."

"You mean she can't remember it happening?" Petra jerked, aghast. "She doesn't know anything about it at all?"

"Not a thing, which is most certainly all for the best. And probably she never will remember." She spoke cheerfully, as if it were a blessing in disguise that the terrible events of the morning should be a complete blank in the muddled mind of the old woman. "So if you have anything to add about the accident, Miss Cunningham, I'd be grateful. The gentleman who called the ambulance said she just seemed to stagger and fall, and someone else who was also in the vicinity seemed to agree with him."

So Bonner had stuck to his story. An accident, with Simon to corroborate what he said. And Mother Carey's mind was a complete blank. What then was the use, Petra thought despairingly. What would be gained by casting suspicion and doubt. Her word against that of Bonner and Simon? And it could have been an accident. After the events of the past week, after the stark terror of that eerie singing, the disembodied laughter, wouldn't she be in a state of mind to believe just about anything?

"That's right," she heard herself reply dully. "She just seemed to fall." She hated herself for what she was saying, but a denial would only serve to start an enquiry that could do nothing but cause distress to a feeble old woman whose mind was now a merciful blank. "It was all over in a flash ..."

"Well, then." The voice was cheerful again. "That's all right. And don't worry about your friend. She will be well cared for."

Yes. Mother Carey would be warm, now, and well-fed. It had all happened for the best.

"Why don't you come in and see her, Miss Cunningham? Hospital patients do so look forward to visitors, you know," the lilting voice urged. "Evenings at seven-thirty. I'll tell her you'll be coming, shall I?"

"No! Don't do that." Petra's voice was sharper than she intended. "No, I can't you see. I'm going back to London, tomorrow – early. It won't be possible, I'm afraid."

"Ah, well, never mind. I'll tell her you were asking after her."

"Yes please. But she doesn't know my name, you see. Perhaps she will understand if you tell her that I am the one who lives in Eleri's house. And tell her, will you, that I am looking after Eleri's doll?"

"And will she understand?" The nurse's voice was indulgent.

"Yes, as far as she is able, I think she will, Sister."

Long after she had laid down the receiver, Petra stood in the roadside kiosk with the wind blowing through a broken pane, spattering her feet with icy drops of rain.

I am going back to London, she thought. Tomorrow. The words had tumbled out without thought or effort, as if she had known all along that that was what she had intended.

Leaving *Ty Mawr*? Leaving the benign old house, the mountains, the peace? Leaving Gareth?

"Oh, no," she whispered to the darkness around her. "I didn't mean it. I didn't mean it ..."

But even as she said the words, she knew that she did. She was running away. Now, when it would be so easy to put things right with the villagers, she was turning her back on the valley. But it was, she conceded dully as a fierce, hopeless pain tore through her, the only sensible thing to do.

She took a long breath, hunched her shoulders against the wind, and set out for the quarry.

She was grateful for the warmth that reached out to her when she returned to *Ty Mawr*. Standing quietly for a moment, she listened to the sounds that an old house makes as it settles down for the night. Almost as if it were sighing, 'Another day gone ...'

Dear *Ty Mawr*, she thought. Old and solid and safe, yet only half a house because it cried out to be lived in, properly lived in by a man and a woman and children. And a dog and a cat, too, and all the things necessary for the turning of a house into a home.

And now, old house, I am going to leave you, Petra thought sadly. I am going back to London to work things out. In London, I will be able to think coherently. I shall not moon about, lovesick and jumpy, hoping to see Gareth Davies walking towards me at every corner I turn. I shall not live in the shadow of Eleri's memory, always guessing, never knowing.

She shook herself mentally and physically and made for the kitchen. There were things to be done, and quickly, before she had the chance to change her mind, but first she was hungry. Hurriedly she heated a tin of soup and cut a hunk of cheese. There were cases to be packed, letters to write to Megan and Bill Jones Post Office and there was Eleri's doll. Always Petra's wayward thoughts returned to the doll. Mother Carey had tried to tell her something. In her half-crazed fashion, she had tried to communicate. Now, Petra admitted, there was little chance of ever learning the truth from the old woman. Gwenny Carey remembered nothing of what had happened that morning. Likely, her muddled old mind had finally given up and pulled down a curtain on the past.

"But you tried to tell me," Petra whispered, "and I've got to know!" And only Eleri's doll, now, might help.

Leaving her food half eaten, she hurried to the locked room, to where she had laid the doll and the pictures, clucking impatiently as yet again the crude drawings refused to give up their secret.

Petra reached out for the doll and carefully removed the hat, examining it painstakingly. It yielded nothing. Nor did the tiny pinafore, the dress or the daintily-sewn underclothes. The legs and arms were carefully attached to the body, but the legs were rigid and only the arms were moveable. The face had been carefully, almost expertly carved. The paint on the red cheeks was cracked with time but unfaded. The neck was long and slender and –

Her heart gave a skip of hope. Around the base of the neck was a thin, even line, almost as if the head had been separately made and glued on – no, *screwed* on! Tapping the body, she gave a cry of delight. Without a doubt, it was hollow. The head *was* meant to unscrew. Heart thumping she grasped it firmly in her hand, easing it anti-clockwise and grunted with triumph as it slowly began to turn.

Why, oh why hadn't she thought of it before? Her mouth was dry with excitement as her probing finger dislodged a tightly folded piece of paper. Eleri had left a letter!

The notepaper on which it was written was pale blue, the writing faded but readable. It was a part of a letter, a sheet torn in two. One side only of the paper had been used and the script that covered it closely was small and even. Tilting it to the light, Petra began to read.

There was no mistaking what those mean little words intended to convey. Only an insensitive fool could fail to grasp their implication.

"No!" Petra whispered. "Oh, no."

She read the letter again and foolish tears pricked her eyes. Poor, unhappy Eleri. The Coroner had returned a verdict of Misadventure, but the small piece of paper in her hand proved otherwise, Petra thought, grimly. Eleri had walked deliberately into the cold, dark lake, there could be no doubting it, and she had done it because ...

Petra jumped to her feet. The piece of paper was an obscenity in her hands. She wanted to tear it across and across and throw the pieces to the wind that moaned outside. But she folded it carefully instead and laid it aside, instinct insisting that it was not hers to destroy. That piece of paper, she acknowledged sadly, had the power to set

Gareth Davies free, but in so doing, it would turn a knife in Megan Pritchard's heart and besmirch Eleri's memory for all time.

Sadly she screwed back the head of the doll, returning the stare of the unseeing eyes. Eleri had no secrets, now. Petra knew what Mother Carey had wanted to tell her and there was nothing she could do about it. Eleri had taken her own life, yet Gareth could never know the reason for that self-destruction. Gareth's pride had already taken too much punishment. To set the seal on Eleri's betrayal would be too cruel. Far better, Petra thought, that she should go back to London. If she had had any doubts about returning, they were dispelled, now. There was nothing for her here, in the valley. The finding of the letter made it only too certain. Slowly she fastened on the tiny garments and tied the tall hat beneath the wooden chin, then laying the doll gently on the bed, snapped off the light and turned the key in the lock behind her.

I wore this coat the night I met Gareth, Petra mused, lifting the cream-coloured garment from the wardrobe and laying it on the bed beside the open case. She had worn it again to Sunday chapel and now it was red-stained and spoiled by the paint that had daubed her car. *Go home, Judas.*

"One ruined coat," she whispered. "Ah, well. Chalk it up to experience, Petra girl."

Carefully she placed tissue paper between the folds of the long, tartan kilt she had worn to the *Noson Lawen*. It was a wonderful evening, she remembered fondly, with everyone laughing and happy and a welcome so warm she wanted to weep with the happiness of belonging. And she had danced with Gareth Davies, danced closely.

"Hell!" Petra jerked. Packing her cases was like packing away her life. Almost every piece of clothing held a memory and here she was, laying them flat and lifeless between layers of soft paper and shutting down the lid on them. Just like Eleri's room of memories, she thought sadly.

But I have to pack away my memories, she insisted. I have to be sensible, think things out, ask the advice of Uncle Ifor's solicitors, and take it. *Ty Mawr* is a wonderful old house and the valley is peaceful and exciting and beautiful, its people friendly. Yet those people turned in an instant, united in their betrayal, and the happiness vanished like midsummer snow, Petra thought wretchedly. I wanted to be part of the valley, learn its language and its customs. I thought Gareth would come to love me as I love him, but I reckoned without Simon's underhandedness and I didn't know that the memory of Eleri could wreak such havoc. And it might have been so wonderful, she yearned. Oh, it wasn't really possible to love someone as she loved Gareth after so short a time. It happened in films, in books, not in real life, she told herself crossly. Her feelings for Gareth Davies were those of attraction, not love. She had felt his nearness, his lips hard on hers, and because she was young and eager with blood that throbbed hotly through her veins, she wanted him as she had never wanted Simon.

But she would get over him. She would soon get into the London swim again and she would forget *Ty Mawr*, in time. It shouldn't be too hard for her to put it on the market then. The old house would make a beautiful home, for the right people. And they *must* be the right people, she insisted. They must undertake that nothing was to be changed, that the house and land must never be sold to a developer who would flood the valley and turn it into a lido. Megan and Tommy and Myfi would understand, in time.

Snapping shut the larger of her two cases, Petra carried it downstairs into the hall. She felt better, now. Calmer and more sensible. Walking through the dining-room to Uncle Ivor's snug little winter-parlour, she sat down at the desk and drew out a sheet of notepaper. To Bill Jones Post Office she wrote that she was returning to London for a time – Myfi would appreciate that. Myfi liked being first with the news – and would he continue to collect the cottage rents and pay them over to her Uncle Ifor's solicitors, expenses paid and commission deducted, of course? And would he be kind enough to pay Megan's wages, each week? Then, after sending good wishes to himself and to Myfi, just as if nothing untoward had ever happened between the village and herself, she signed the letter with a flourish and sealed it inside a matching envelope.

She thought a lot before beginning her letter to Megan Pritchard. She tore up her first attempt because it sounded too formal and the second because it sounded trite and uncaring. Eventually she wrote,

Dear Megan,

I am leaving early tomorrow for London and I am not yet sure when I will be back.

The future of *Ty Mawr* is very important to me and I would like a little time away, to think things out.

Rest assured that when I come to a decision, you will be the first to hear of it, and meantime, I know you will take good care of *Ty Mawr* for me for a little while longer.

Thank you for all you have done in the past.

With fondest good wishes,

Yours,

Petra.

Sighing gently, she closed the desk and turned out the light. She felt neither sad nor happy, now, just curiously numb, relieved that she was doing the right thing.

Checking windows and doors, placing the guard over the dying embers of the sitting-room fire, she walked through the house for the last time, turning out lights as she went.

It hadn't been too bad, she thought, coming to a decision. Once she had taken herself in hand and faced facts like a reasonable adult, it hadn't hurt too much.

"No one can have everything she wants in this life," she whispered to her reflection in the dressing-table mirror, "and I am lucky. I have more than most. I'll forget the valley. It isn't for me. I'll forget the sound of the river and the clear, sweet air and it won't be too hard to stop thinking about Gareth Davies, because it isn't real love I feel for him. It can't be. I shall forget him, in time ...

Petra awoke to birdsong and the half light of a dawn that promised a bright, sunny day. The fingers of the bedside clock pointed to four-thirty.

If I get up now, she reasoned, flinging aside the bedclothes and groping for her slippers, I can be well on my way before anyone is about.

Now the time had come, she wanted to be gone. No sense in delaying. Just a quick shower and a mug of coffee. The petrol tank was full, there was nothing to stop her going. There would be no last looks, no regrets. She would not look back.

The chapel clock was striking six as she parked her car in the village square. Carefully, she pushed Bill Jones Post Office's letter under the door of Myfi's General Store, then crossed the road and pushed the envelope addressed to

Megan through the letter-box. It fell to the floor with a plop, but no dog barked and no light appeared at any bedroom window.

Thankfully, Petra drove away, turning back in her tracks, heading for the valley road. She was going out of her way, but perhaps she would allow herself one last look at *Ty Mawr* below her, one fleeting glimpse of *Ty Coch*, the squat little farmhouse with the red-painted doors.

When she reached the widening in the road where cars or carts could pass in safety, Petra drew to a halt and looked down into the valley. To her left stood *Ty Mawr*, with the river sparkling past it and below her, gentled by the rising sun, lay Gareth's farm. As she watched, a thin spiral of smoke drifted upwards then she heard the urgent barking of a dog. Gareth was lighting his fire, had let Gyp loose for his morning run. Soon, he would bring in the cows for morning milking and it would be so easy to linger for a while, to watch unseen as he climbed to the pasture, Gyp beside him, to call down the beasts.

"Cush, cush, cush. Cush, pet ..."

They would lumber towards him, Gyp slinking at their heels and another day would begin for Gareth Davies; another lonely day.

Quickly Petra turned the ignition key, then without looking behind her, swung out onto the track again, pulling the back of her glove across her eyes impatiently.

"I am *not* crying," she whispered. I am *not* unhappy to be leaving the valley. *Ty Mawr* is only a house and there are many more villages, for the finding. And I *don't* care about Gareth Davies. It's only that he attracted me a little. I never loved him, not really."

And she didn't care. Really she didn't, and the sound in her ears was not the sound of sobbing ...

Twelve

Petra made good time to Shrewsbury. Through the open window of her car the early morning breeze whipped at her hair and set a flush glowing in her cheeks. She was glad, she told herself, that she had made the break with the minimum amount of fuss; glad to have been able to tear herself away from the influence of the valley; glad she had had the sound common sense to realise that she could not possibly have loved Gareth Davies. What she felt for him was attraction, surely? Love, *real* love, couldn't seed and flourish in one short week – could it?

She felt the need for a cup of strong, sweet coffee and drank it in a black-timbered tea shop in the ages-old town. They would be surprised to see her at the flat, she realised as she munched a sweet, curranty biscuit. She would be staying in Wales, she had told them, for at least two weeks, and they would demand to know why she had cut short her holiday and ask a hundred and one other questions that she had no wish to answer.

Yes, she would tell them, *Ty Mawr* was indeed a lovely old house, larger and lonelier than she had ever envisaged. Of course the countryside around was beautiful and of course it had been very hard to tear herself away, but they must understand, she would stress, that the decision to change her whole way of living was one that must be given a great deal of thought.

And what would she tell them about Gareth Davies when they demanded to know the density of marriageable males per acre? Would she shrug him off with a laugh?

"Well, yes, there *was* a farmer. Tall and dark and brooding – a sort of Welsh Heathcliff, yearning for his Eleri – but I saw very little of him ..."

No, she couldn't tell them about Gareth. She couldn't tolerate their smiles and glances and twittering innuendoes. And she wouldn't tell them about the voices or the laughter or anything at all about Eleri. Eleri was dead and she, Petra, knew now what lay behind the guarded eyes. She was the keeper of Eleri's secret and no one would ever see the small piece of pale-blue notepaper that lay folded in her purse.

She would not think of Eleri, yet Eleri was still in Petra's thoughts as she sped through the beautiful Worcester countryside, pink over with drifts of apple-blossom. And Gareth, whom she didn't really love, and who should be so easy to forget, was in her mind as she pressed on towards Gloucester and the quaint and lovely villages of the Cotswolds. But the beauty of it all was lost upon her, because beauty was always the better for being shared, she sighed, and she was alone, alone in every way. A familiar sadness ripped through her like a physical pain and she wanted to cry out against it.

She was nearing London and now that the valley was far behind her, now that she had passed the point of no return, Petra had a primaeval urge to settle back into the flat, to shut *Ty Mawr* out of her mind completely and pick up the pieces of her life as once it had been.

At Oxford she stopped only long enough to fill the tank with petrol and one o'clock saw her at the outskirts of London. In little over an hour, she would be safely back at the flat, her cases unpacked, and there would be time before Penny and Iris returned to rein in her wayward thoughts, take a firm grip on her emotions and prepare to meet the verbal onslaught of their curiosity.

But the little attic flat, when she entered it, had an unnaturally deserted air about it. For one thing, it was far too tidy. Mail lay uncollected behind the door, coffee mugs hung clean from their hooks whilst the bathroom looked unusually bereft, bare of dripping tights and panties. There was no milk in the fridge, no biscuits in the tin and the little white cage that housed Penny's pet bird was missing from the window-sill.

The caretaker, who lived in the basement flat and who knew everything about everybody who lived in the house, explained away the mystery as he filled Petra's jug with milk.

"Just handed me Sweetie Pie," he said, nodding to the white cage on the sideboard, "and said they'd be back Friday night. Got the chance to share a cottage for a week down Eastbourne way and off they went on Sunday morning."

"And didn't they leave an address?"

"Not them, Miss. Not those two. Still," he beamed, "it'll be nice and quiet for a few days, eh?"

He tapped his nose with his forefinger and nodded his head and she knew he was thinking about Simon.

She smiled and thanked him and said nothing. Come to think of it, there was nothing now she need say. Glad of the respite, grateful that she would be able to think things over without emotion or coercion, she closed the door behind her.

The little living-room with its low ceiling and sloping walls closed in on her and she recalled the high, wide hall at *Ty Mawr*, the tall windows, the lofty rooms.

"Leave me alone?" she whispered, shutting down her thoughts, blotting out the dear familiar picture, the sound of creaking doors and ticking clocks, the remembered smell of blazing logs and beeswax polish.

Clucking impatiently she carried the kettle to the tap. Through the tiny window she saw a sweep of rooftops with chimneys, higgledy-piggledy and soot-stained, belching smoke and grime, and it reminded her of the hills that were clean and bare and snow-tipped, still.

There was a plane tree in the courtyard below, its maple-like leaves unmoving in the still air, its trunk rough with peeling bark, and she saw instead the gentle willows, bending towards the bright water and the beech leaves, hardly unfolded, innocently, tenderly green.

Petra set the kettle on the stove top with unnecessary force. Forgetting *Ty Mawr* wasn't going to be easy. How was she to stop thinking about the mountains, the greenness of the grass, the sparkle of Spring? How could she blot out the sense of belonging, the lilting, laughing way the valley people spoke, the unhurried pace of life, there? When would she learn to think of Gareth with a steady heart? Would she ever learn to stop caring? Never, supplied her heart dully and in that moment she knew that no matter how hard she tried to delude herself, she would love him beyond all time.

"All right, Gareth Davies, you win," she whispered, suddenly fiercely proud. "I love you and I'll never forget you, but I'll not share you with Eleri. And until you can

love me the way I love you, you can live with your stiff-
necked pride and your memories, and see if I care!' "

But she did care and she closed her eyes against tears
that all too readily flowed hotly down her cheeks.

"But I will learn to live without him," she vowed. "As
from now, I *will* learn."

For the first two days, Petra worked hard around the
little flat, occupying her mind with ordinary things so that
pictures of the valley might not intrude. She washed panties
and tights and blouses and festooned them about the
bathroom with a grunt of satisfaction. She bundled up
bedding and towels and carried them to the launderette,
sitting with eyes focused on the twirling suds. She swept
and polished until her bones protested, then fell into bed
exhausted, to lie wide-eyed, straining to hear the call of the
owl, the river-sounds, the far away bark of a dog called
Gyp.

She awoke to bright sunlight, determined to fill the
remaining days of her holiday to the utmost. She had
always promised herself a trip to Kew, a visit to the Tower
and Hampton Court. And the London parks were at their
loveliest, now. There was so much to see and do. She would
cram each day with activity, so that there would be no time
to think. Soon, next week, perhaps, she really would try to
come to a decision. When the hurt had gone and the pain
inside her had receded, then she would be better able to
think sensibly. Uncle Ifor's lawyers were there to help her –
she must tell them about the development company, insist
that if *Ty Mawr* was sold, it should be left intact. No one
must be allowed to destroy the village or flood the valley.
The old house must not be submerged beneath –

She was thinking about the valley again. It seemed that

in every unguarded moment it called to her, that even above
the traffic din she could hear the cry of water-birds on the
river bank and the screech of the night owl. It was as if *Ty
Mawr* reached out, urging her back and she in return felt a
yearning that tingled to the tips of her toes and refused to
be pacified.

She fought that yearning to the limit of her being. She
visited Kew and Hampton Court and the Tower. She
window-shopped in Bond Street and mixed with pigeon-
snapping tourists in Trafalgar Square, but there was an air
of unreality about it all. It was as if, she conceded, her body
was here in London and her heart and mind were in Wales,
drinking in the sights and sounds, roaming free beneath the
wide, clear sky.

On the morning of the day on which Iris and Penny were
due to return, Petra sat in St James' Park and threw
crumbs to a squabble of fearless little sparrows. She had
watched the fluffy ducklings, smiling at their endearing
antics and feeling a wave of tenderness wash over her as it
always did when she looked at something little and helpless
and innocent. There were wild mallards on the riverbank
beside *Ty Mawr*. She had seen the pairing of the brightly
coloured drakes and the drab little ducks and now she
wondered how soon it would be before the cheep of
ducklings would be heard there.

"I am thinking again," she told herself resignedly. "The
valley – it won't be shut out ..."

A child was playing on the grass beside her, a child with
a lilting voice, a Welsh voice. It called out to the woman
who sat at the other end of the bench and Petra's heart
warmed to the sing-song syllables.

"Don't you go getting lost, now! Do you hear what your
Mam says, *cariad*?"

Cariad. Gareth had said that word. That afternoon when they stood on the plateau and looked down on *Ty Coch*. He had gathered her in his arms and his kiss had been desperate and pleading.

"Oh, Petra. Petra, *cariad* ..."

Petra smiled at the red-cheeked woman.

"You're from Wales?" she asked.

"There now – and how did you know?"

"I suppose you might say that I'm half Welsh myself."

"Oh, yes? And whereabouts would your Welsh half come from?"

She shuffled up the bench, her eyes showing interest. Like Myfi Chester did.

"From Gwynedd – Caernarvon way."

"Oh, I went to Caernarvon on a day-trip with the chapel, once. I'm from Anglesey myself. Stopping with my brother in London for a few days, and fair exhausted I am."

"You've been seeing the sights?"

"Oh, it isn't that so much, as the rushing. Rush, rush everywhere, it is. No time for a chat and everybody with their doors shut and minding their own business like it was a new religion." She stopped short and blushed. "Now, there's me talking out of the top of my head. I'm not criticising, not really. I'm getting a bit homesick, I think." She smiled suddenly then said brightly. "Well, I'm going home tomorrow ..."

Going home, Petra thought as the yearning tugged at her heart again. Tomorrow. Going home to Wales.

"Do you speak Welsh?" Petra asked, amazed at the trembling in her voice.

"Oh, yes. In Anglesey it's our mother-tongue. The English comes to us later, in dribs and drabs, like. What makes you ask, lovely?"

"It was a word you used – when you were calling to your little girl. *Cariad.* What does it mean?"

"Well now, that all depends." The woman pursed her lips and frowned. "It's like this, see? You say it to a child, like I did, and it might mean *pet*, or *my dear*. It's an affectionate word, if you get my meaning?"

"And if a man said it?" Petra prompted.

"Ah, now." The dark eyes twinkled and the mobile mouth curved into a smile. "There's different. When your young man says it to you it means what you want it to mean, like *dear one*, perhaps, or *darling* or *beloved*. It's a lovely word, is *cariad*." Her eyes shone tenderly. "Oh, yes ..."

Petra smiled. It was indeed a lovely word. And suddenly the bustle about her was stilled and the traffic noises hushed and she heard again the valley sounds, clear and unmistakable. The yearning possessed her completely and Gareth was whispering in her ear, "Oh, Petra, *cariad* ..." And the voices of the valley took up the pleading and it swelled to a great crescendo until it was like a roaring in her ears.

"Come home. Come home."

Never had Petra felt so free. Never, in the whole of her life, had she been so sure about anything. She was going back to the valley, to the high hills, to the sweet green pastures and the bright, unsullied air. She was going home, to *Ty Mawr*.

Her letters were written. One to Iris and Penny, the other to her employers. She still had holidays due to her and she asked that they would accept them in lieu of her notice. Unethical, perhaps, disloyal maybe, but the call of the valley was too strong and she could do nothing but obey it blindly.

The flat looked like a rumpus room. As many clothes and personal belongings as she could carry were packed and ready to stow away in the little car. The remainder were piled on her bed to be collected later, or sent on by rail. Her heart was beating loudly, great happy thumps that echoed in her ears and made her feel light-headed.

The fingers of the clock pointed to four. She threw biscuits and apples into a bag and poured cold milk into a vacuum flask, then slamming the door behind her she ran quickly down the stairs. Two hours later, London was far behind her.

Through the open car window the breeze teased her new hair-do. She breathed deeply, calmer now, no longer afraid that something would happen to delay her flight. She was well on her way, and nothing, no one, could stop her. By midnight, with luck, she would be back again. Tonight, she would lie beneath *Ty Mawr's* sagging old roof and the river would sing her to sleep. Foolish, happy tears filled her eyes and she blinked them away. The car engine purred sweetly in the early evening air and the miles sped past.

"Home," she whispered. "I'm going home."

The waning moon cast long shadows and the stars were so bright in the dark blue sky that it seemed they had been polished especially for her return. Below her, in the dip, stood *Ty Mawr*, and to her right Petra could make out the squat, blurred outline of *Ty Coch*. No lights shone from its windows, for the valley was asleep.

She had driven in on the high road then turned at the crossroads and passed through the shuttered village.

"And not even .Myfi Chester has seen me," Petra laughed.

She recalled Myfi's bitter outburst and wondered how long it would be before the villagers accepted that she wasn't going to sell up and that the way of life of the valley would not be disturbed.

"Oh, please let them like me again?" she prayed quietly.

And what of Gareth? Loving him as she did, how hard would it be to keep Eleri's secret? She could show him that torn page and when the pain of knowing had lessened, at least his pride could begin to heal once more. But what of Megan Pritchard, Petra fretted. Kind, comfortable Megan who had taken Eleri for her own and reared her with love. Megan must never know. The verdict of 'Misadventure' the Coroner had returned must stand. There was no doubt about it whatever.

Petra shook her head as if to rid it of unhappy thoughts. This was her homecoming, and nothing should be allowed to spoil it.

She dropped a gear and nosed the car between the tall gateposts. Turning the key in the ignition, she wound down the window and relaxed in her seat. Gradually, her ears became attuned to the stillness and she heard once more the murmur of the river and the frightened cry of a little hunted creature. The night owl ghosted above her on wide, silent wings.

Petra reached for the heavy old key. It had lay on the seat beside her like a talisman and now, in just a few seconds, she would unlock the iron-studded door. Happiness wrapped around her like a soft, warm cloak as she gazed upwards at the criss-crossed window panes, reflecting the starlight and it seemed as if they were benign old eyes, shining a welcome, smiling knowingly, as if they had always known she would return.

Petra smiled back then placed the key in the lock with trembling fingers. Things would work out, she was sure of it.

Thirteen

Not to be outdone by the shining stars, the sun beamed an early morning welcome into Petra's sleep-heavy eyes. She looked at her watch. It was eight o'clock and someone was walking along the passage outside. There was a discreet cough, a tap on the door, then Megan stood there, a tray in her hands and a smile on her face that put the sunlight to shame.

"Well now, you're back."

She set down the tray then stood, her eyes wary, asking mutely that she should be met half way.

"Megan, oh, Megan!" Petra sprang out of bed and threw her arms around the older woman. "I'm forgiven, then? Everything's all right again?"

"Everything's all right," she nodded, her dark eyes serious, "and there's nothing to forgive. When we realised you weren't going to sell, that you weren't hand-in-glove with Bonner and the man from London, we felt very ashamed of ourselves, especially Myfi Chester. Always going off like a fire-cracker, is Myfi ..."

"It doesn't matter." Petra picked up the tea-tray. "Look, let's go downstairs? What say you cook me some breakfast? I'm starving. I really am."

Megan's face brightened visibly and she followed Petra

who ran ahead lightheartedly, her bare feet pattering down the long slate passage that led to the kitchen.

"Right!" Petra smiled, drawing up a chair. "I'll have bacon and egg and fried bread – lashings of fried bread – and thick, buttered toast to follow. And will you tell me, please, just how you knew I was here? I was so sure no one had seen me."

"Ah, but the postman saw you. Noticed your car outside when he brought the mail in at half past six, this morning. Well, he told Myfi, didn't he, and Myfi rushed across to tell me. So I filled up a basket, and here I am – or at least here *we* are." She pointed to Moggy's basket where a tiny black kitten slept contentedly, its fat little stomach rising and falling rhythmically.

"That's Little Moggy. I brought him with me this morning to show you. You can have him for keeps as soon as he's properly house-trained."

"Why, Megan, what a lovely thought. You must have known all along I would come back."

"We all hoped you would, Miss Petra. Oh, it was a shock, seeing you with the man from London. When I realised he was your boyfriend, I thought the worst. We all did. We knew someone had been trying to buy *Ty Mawr* for a long time. I suppose it was natural to think the worst."

"Well, he's not my boyfriend any more. He didn't really think anything about me, you know. When he learned from Uncle Ifor that *Ty Mawr* would be mine one day, he made it his business to get to know me. I suppose he thought it would be easy, once I inherited, to persuade me to sell."

"But you won't sell?"

"No, Megan, but how I'm going to manage, I don't know."

"You need a man about the place," Megan turned the

toast with studied nonchalance, "and I could name you half
a dozen young men from around these parts who'd give a
lot to get their hands on *Ty Mawr* land. They'd make it pay,
all right."

Petra sipped her tea thoughtfully, nodding her head as if
in agreement, saying nothing.

"But farm hands cost money," Megan continued
comfortably, "so the best thing you can do, Miss Petra, is to
find yourself a husband."

"And how do I set about it, do you suppose?" Petra's
voice was light but her cheeks flamed hotly. "Tell Myfi
Chester I'm in the market for a well set-up farmer, or would
it sound better if Mr Gruffydd announced it from the pulpit
next Sunday?"

"Gareth Davies needs a wife." Assiduously Megan
ignored Petra's remarks. "Gareth's a good man, a fine
man." She set a plate before Petra. "Take care, now. It's
hot."

"Gareth Davies wouldn't marry me if I were the only
woman left in Gwynedd and besides, there's Eleri."

"Eleri's dead, poor lamb."

"But Gareth won't marry until he knows the truth of it.
He thinks that Eleri took her life rather than marry him,
and that's a lot for a man like Gareth Davies to accept."

"You understand him, don't you *merchi*? And I think
you're fond of him, too."

Petra nodded mutely. It was one thing to try to deceive
herself, but it seemed as if Megan's dark eyes were looking
deep into her soul. Deceiving Megan was quite another
thing.

"Then you'd better go to him, girl, for he'll not come to
you, that's for sure. Even now that he knows, he's too proud
to – "

"Knows what?" Petra's mouth was suddenly dry and she pushed aside her plate, the food on it untouched. "Tell me?"

For just a moment Megan Pritchard hesitated, then taking a deep breath and pulling out a chair she whispered,

"Mind if I sit down, *merchi*? Yesterday I told the truth of it to Gareth and you must know, too. It's been heavy on my conscience for a long time. Best get it over with."

She sat down heavily and folded her arms on the table-top, her eyes staring ahead, troubled and sad.

"They said it was an accident. 'Misadventure' the Coroner gave out, after the post-mortem. But Eleri had reason enough for taking her life. She was going to have a baby ..."

Petra closed her eyes and swallowed hard, then said quietly,

"How long have you known, Megan?"

"I've always known. About a month after Eleri died, I think it was that I found out. Your uncle told me. 'Megan', he said to me one morning – I'd been weeping again, and it showed, I suppose, 'Megan, there's no use grieving over Eleri. It's what she wanted. She'd never have had any peace'. And then he told me she'd been three months pregnant."

"But how did Uncle Ifor know, and not you, Megan? Surely Eleri would have told you?"

"Eleri told nobody. It was the man who did the post-mortem who told your uncle. Friends, they'd always been, you see. Known Eleri, too, since she was a babe, that old doctor had. We were lucky. The regular man, the – " She shook her head, searching for the correct word.

"Pathologist?"

"Yes, that's it," Megan nodded, her eyes unmoving.

"Well, the hospital pathologist was away and it was your Uncle Ifor's friend who was standing in for him – *locum* – is that it?"

"Yes, that's right," Petra said softly.

"Well, this friend was a retired doctor. Lucky, maybe, or perhaps it was meant to be. Anyway, that doctor did something that most people would think was very wrong. His report, when he made it, had no mention in it of Eleri being pregnant. It wasn't a criminal thing to do, your uncle said. Unethical, maybe, but it protected Eleri and it harmed nobody. And it wasn't as if her life had been insured, or anything. They do that, in the valley, you know. Protect their own ..."

"And who knew about it?"

"Just your uncle and the pathologist and me, that's all. The doctor's long dead, rest his kind old soul, so there's only you and me that knows – and Gareth, of course. Gareth knows, now."

"How did he take it?" Petra whispered.

"Better than I thought he would. I asked him outright. 'Gareth', I said, 'did you have any idea? Had you any cause to think Eleri might be having a baby?' Well, I couldn't put it any plainer, could I? And he said he hadn't. Hadn't even suspected. So then I asked him outright if it could have been his child and he told me it couldn't be. 'Not any way,' he said, and I believed him. All those years of wondering, yet I never thought that Gareth would – "

Her voice trailed into a whisper, and Petra knew a moment of panic. It would be so easy to say, "But I know, Megan. Eleri left a letter ..." So easy, yet she must not. Best leave it.

"And have you any ideas of your own?" Petra asked, her heart beating so loudly that she was certain Megan must hear it. "Have you the least suspicion?"

"None at all, and I don't want to know who the man was. Better that I shouldn't," she said, gently. "Best not torture myself, I decided. Let the poor child rest. I don't think ill of her. She did what she did because of the shame, you see. There'd have been talk in the valley and pointing fingers and sly looks. She couldn't have taken that." She sighed loudly and the sound of it tore at Petra's heart. "All the same, I'll never know why she didn't tell Gareth. You'd have thought she'd have confided in him, wouldn't you?"

She dabbed at her eyes with the corner of her pinafore, then smiling gently said,

"So you'd best be taking a walk up to *Ty Coch*, Miss Petra. Like I said, Gareth Davies has been lonely long enough and now that he knows the truth about Eleri, now that he has nothing to blame himself for ..."

"I will," Petra smiled. "I will."

"Not before you've eaten your breakfast," Megan scolded, mistress in her own kitchen once more, "and anyway, he's gone to market, this morning. Now, most evenings he goes up to the plateau, if the weather is fine. Takes Gyp with him, walks his land. Maybe if you were to go up there a bit later, eh?"

"Perhaps," Petra affirmed. "Perhaps I just will, Megan ..."

It was early evening, long after Megan had left, with Little Moggy protesting loudly from the bicycle basket, that Petra walked along the upstairs passage to the room that was always closed, to Eleri's room, the shrine of Ifor Jones's making. But there was no key in the lock and when she turned the handle Petra was surprised that the door opened without effort. Shocked, she stood on the threshold, staring into the ordinary room, with rose-sprigged curtains and bedcover that had been freshly laundered and windows opened wide to the spring sunshine. Gone were the books, the toys, the desk. Gone were the clothes, the shoes, the wedding dress and the bridal veil and on the bow-fronted chest, where she had left the pictures and the wooden-faced doll, stood a bowl of primroses, sweet and fresh as a new beginning. Eleri had gone from *Ty Mawr*. Gently and sadly, Megan had banished her.

"So now," Petra whispered, "there is only one more thing to be done."

Slowly she returned to the sitting-room and from her purse she took the torn half-sheet of pale blue notepaper. Her mouth watered with distaste as she read, for the last time, the words that had driven Eleri Pritchard despairingly to the dark water.

... and there is nothing I can do about it since I am not the marrying kind. You should know that, Eleri. I told you often enough. Why don't you kid Gareth Davies that the baby is his? He would believe anything you told him. Thanks for everything. It was fun, while it lasted ...

Petra reached out for the matchbox that lay on the hearth, holding the paper between her thumb and forefinger, regarding it distastefully for a little while as if it were contaminated. Then deliberately she held a match flame to it, watching fascinated as it blazed and blackened and withered.

"It's all right now, Eleri," she whispered to the empty room. "No one will ever know. Not Gareth, not even Megan."

Eleri had placed the letter inside the wooden doll and

given it to Mother Carey the night before she died. But the old woman did not find that letter, and if she had, it would have been to no avail, for in her distress, Eleri had forgotten that Mother Carey knew no English. And now Eleri's secret was doubly safe, because the old woman lay in a hospital bed, her mind a blank and ever likely to remain so. Only *he* knew, the man who without love had fathered Eleri's child, the man whose initials sat smugly on the bottom of the letter, and he would never tell. Edward Bonner would never dare risk the wrath of the valley ...

She sighed. Soon the sun would sink below the hills and a lonely man would whistle to his dog and walk the boundaries of his farm. Gently Petra smiled, and closed the window.

The evening sky was tinged with lavender, the clouds pink-tipped.

"Red sky at night. Shepherds' delight," Petra chanted, slipping a jacket over her dress and pushing her feet into flat, sturdy shoes.

As she crossed the hall she stopped and looked at herself frankly in the mirror. Her face, newly washed in rainwater, was bare of makeup, her cheeks were flushed, her eyes shining.

She closed the door behind her then started to climb, upwards toward the soaring cliff top and the lush green plateau beyond it. Somewhere up there, she hoped, Gareth might be walking his land with Gyp at his heels. Somewhere beyond the crags she might see him again, his hair wind-tousled, his dark eyes deep and watchful. What would she say to him when they met? What would he say to her?

She paused for breath and glanced down. Below, with

woodsmoke rising from one of its chimneys, lay *Ty Mawr*, safe and secure. Around the bluff, set a little higher, would be *Ty Coch*, Gareth's red house, and soon, when she reached the top and the path that ran along it, she would be able to look across to the plateau and maybe he would be there, waiting. And if he wasn't there?

"Then I will wait for him," Petra whispered.

She saw him, a long way off and her heart gave a joyful lurch. He was turned away from her, looking down towards *Ty Coch* and the dark water below it.

Petra called his name and the wind swept it along. She saw Gyp scramble to his feet, head cocked, then Gareth spun round and stood motionless, staring in her direction. She waved her hand, then started to run.

When she was a few yards away from him she stopped, suddenly shy. She tried to speak, but none of the words she could think of seemed the right ones to say. So she smiled and waited for him to speak to her. He said, eventually,

"So you have come back, Petra?"

She nodded. "I didn't mean to. I thought if I tried hard enough, I could forget *Ty Mawr* ..."

"But you couldn't."

"No, Gareth. It was as if there was a voice inside me. I couldn't shut it out. It was always there, calling."

"The hiraeth," he nodded.

"*Hiraeth*?"

They were still standing apart, talking to each other across an invisible barrier.

"It's a word you can't really define. It's a kind of longing, a yearning that reaches out over time and distance and calls you back – back home."

"Then I was suffering from it very badly, Gareth."

"Ah, yes ..."

She looked at him, loving him. He was just as she had

known he would be. His hair was tousled and his eyes were sad with longing. Without moving she said,

"Megan told me you would be here. I came to you, Gareth."

"And she told you? You know about Eleri?"

"I know."

"So you see, I have been very stupid, Petra. I have given away ten precious years because I never imagined for one moment that Eleri had taken her life because she couldn't face – couldn't live with what she had done." Unmoving, he looked at her and his eyes were bleak, his jaw set tight. "I thought it must be something deeper, you see," he continued. "I didn't think it could be anything as basic and ordinary as having a baby. And she didn't tell me, Petra." He dug his hands deep into his pockets then shrugged his shoulders. "She didn't tell me. That's how much faith she had in my love for her. She didn't ask for my understanding because she knew there would be none. I was pretty intolerant, in those days ..."

He turned away from her and it seemed to Petra that the gulf between them was widening. With every second they were drifting farther apart. Soon, the moment would be ended. Soon, the magic that danced between them would be gone, spoiled, borne away beyond the hilltops, out of their reach. Someone had to break down the barrier, cross the divide.

"And you haven't improved much for the keeping, Gareth Davies," she whispered. "You are intolerant, still, and arrogant and prickly and proud and I don't know why I love you. I don't know why I came back to you. I don't know why I can't face another day without you." With a gesture of pleading she raised her head and looked into his eyes. "Gareth, *cariad*?"

Then she was in his arms, her mouth searching

unashamedly for his. She heard the groan that jerked from his throat as their lips met and it sent desire tearing through her like a white-hot flame. She wanted never to let him go, but he lifted his head and pushed her a little way from him, his fingers hurting her arms.

"You said that very well, for an English woman," he whispered, his voice rough. "Do you know what *cariad* means?"

"Yes, Gareth. I think so."

"Then tell me."

"It means you are my sweetheart, my darling, my very dearly beloved. It's the only Welsh word I know."

"It is enough," he smiled. "It is the only one you need ever know."

He placed his hand beneath her chin, tilting it a little so that their eyes met. He said,

"I love you, English woman. I have loved you since you came to me out of the mist, as if you had come from the dark water."

They turned and looked down. Below them, a little lake gently reflected the pinks and purples of the evening sky. For a while they stood, hands clasped, remembering, then folding her gently in his arms once more he whispered,

"Did I tell you that I love you?"

"You did, a minute ago, but say it again, *cariad*. Please say it again?"

Somewhere in the valley below them, the night-bird cried, but they did not hear it.